Roger Bourke White Jr.

Babymaking in the year 2112

AuthorHouse™
1663 Liberty Drive
Bloomington, IN 47403
www.authorhouse.com
Phone: 1-800-839-8640

Published by AuthorHouse 8/9/2012

ISBN: 978-1-4772-5301-4 (sc)
ISBN: 978-1-4772-5300-7 (e)

Library of Congress Control Number: 2012913591

Books by Roger Bourke White Jr.

Tales of Technofiction Series
www.technofictionland.com

The Honeycomb Comet
Rostov Rising
Tips for Tailoring Spacetime Fabric, Vol. 1
Tips for Tailoring Spacetime Fabric, Vol. 2
Science and Insight for Science Fiction Writing

Business and Insight Series
www.cyreenik-says.com

Surfing the High Tech Wave: A History of Novell 1980–1990
Evolution and Thought: Why We Think the Way We Do
How Evolution Explains the Human Condition

Talbe of Contents

Preface

This story is taking place in 2112, and human civilization a hundred years from now will be different in many ways. The goal of this book is to present you, the reader, with an interesting story about what it's going to be like in a future world that is really possible, and really probable.

This is not a post-holocaust or Malthusian-stressed world. It's a comfortable world where mankind has faced our contemporary challenges and found successful solutions.

So... be prepared for a very different kind of story.

Axioms

Let me give you the axioms of the world in this story. These axioms are the "givens" of this world.

> *Earth is a happy and productive place.* The hundred years between now and story time have been filled with people becoming more prosperous and more urbanized. There have been no civilization-disrupting catastrophes.
>
> Earth's human population peaked at about 9 billion in 2050, and by 2112 it is down to about 7 billion and declining steadily. This has happened because prosperous people find they have many interesting things to spend their time on other than baby-making and raising. This is an important point, so I will say it again: The population decline is due

to prosperity and the distractions it brings to people, not due to improvement in birth control, disaster, or some government-imposed, draconian, population-controlling regulation. Because the population is declining due to prosperity, the world is "grayer" than it is today—there are many, many more old people and fewer young people. It is also much more urbanized—90% of the world's human population lives in large metropolitan areas or popular resort areas that service these urban areas. The rest of the world has a lot less people than even today. Small cities and rural areas are virtually depopulated… of people.

The world is much more automated than it is today, and the automation is much more efficient. This has allowed mankind to become more prosperous and more efficient at using Earth's resources—so much more efficient that resource exhaustion is no longer a threat; it is now just a well understood issue. To human eyes, the pinnacle expression of this increased automation is the creations. These are self-aware robots who are part of a self-aware, world-wide network that does both computing and communication. The creations and the less complex, supporting computer systems and communications networks do the routine legwork that keeps civilization prosperous, productive, and operating with a light impact on earth's resources. Creations and other automation infrastructure are now what inhabit the many cities and rural areas that humans have migrated away from.

There are self-aware cyber entities in the global communication/computation network, but their interaction with humans is subtle and happens mostly through creation activities. These are mostly off human radar.

There is some space travel and humans are still steadily getting better at it. Humans routinely travel to the moon and Mars, and creations are exploring the rest of the solar system. The amount of space travel grows as this story is in progress, and it gets easier and faster, and this changes how people live. A handful of explorer probes are en route to other star systems and expect to arrive millennia from now, but that's it for star travel.

There has been a lot of advancement in biological sciences and technologies. These advancements have produced technology surprises. The surprises, and how humans react to them, are much of what these stories are about.

The story that follows presumes all of the above are true. If you feel you have the picture, you can move on to the Prelude now. If you'd like more details about these axioms, keep on reading.

The People

The decline in population will happen not because of a holocaust of any sort or because humans have run out of a vital resource and are now in a Malthusian crisis—a crisis of too many people sharing too few resources. It will happen because 90 percent of the world's population will be living a prosperous urban or suburban lifestyle, and as a result, people are too busy with other enjoyable activities to have enough time and interest to make and raise enough babies.

Prosperous urban lifestyles are fun, interesting, and personally satisfying, but because there are so many interesting things to do, child raising gets put off for years and years, and one or two children are the most common numbers for those who do find the time. After 2050 not *enough* people are spontaneously willing to commit to the long hours and years of dedication it takes to raise children, so the population has been declining for decades. It is now 2112, and this decline has been going on long enough that even the population growth alarmists admit that it's not a fluke.

It is now recognized by most people that without community intervention of some sort, or a catastrophe of some sort that sends most people back to the farm, there will now never be enough children to sustain the population. Steps must be taken to encourage child raising.

Much of this story is about what such steps will be.

However, those people who *do* take on the sacrifice of child bearing and child raising will, as is true today, want the best for those children. In fact, they will want it even more so because there is nothing inevitable about their choice. Another difference is, because they live in a prosperous world, they will have a lot more resource to throw at the adventure.

The Creations

Automation, computers, and communications networks will have continued their exponential growth in both capability and complexity. The result is that productivity of day-to-day goods and services is ten to a thousand times what we experience today. In other words, humanity is ten to ten thousand times more efficient at making stuff. That means that human civilization is no longer taxing earth's resources.

It also means that computers are doing ninety percent or more of the legwork to make manufacturing, transportation, and other routine activities happen. Humans don't make much in this world; they do other things. (What they do is much of what this story is about.)

Humans interact directly with creations. Creations are the middle beings between humans and the vast cyber infrastructure that also inhabits earth and directly handles most of the manufacturing and transportation. Creations are self-aware robots that range from human-looking to quite robotic in form.

As pointed out above, the automation infrastructure is what inhabits much of the world's surface between the densely-human-inhabited metropolitan areas.

(Note: The creations are much more aware of how complex all the earth's computing has become. But this is a story about humans, so we will see the world through their eyes.)

What This Story Is About

This story is a series of tales about people living in the world of 2112.

It's about the surprises we can expect as our human civilization gets more and more prosperous and we learn and exploit deeper and deeper mysteries of science and technology.

Since these stories are about surprises, this book is not some crystal ball telling about exactly what will happen when, but it is about the lifestyles of people that are likely to emerge as the world gets more automated and more prosperous. *It is about how human thinking and living will interact with the opportunities more and more prosperity will give it.*

Let me say that this has been a challenging tale to create—challenging because it's not conventional storytelling. But hopefully, even if it is not a familiar story theme, you will find it enjoyable, interesting, and compelling.

Have fun with... The World of 2112!

Prelude

The Cast

On Earth

Dahlia Rose—Child Champs teacher and viewpoint character

Miranda An—immigrant student from Laos

Janet and Ben Hosker—older retired professional couple

Rubyzin—pop rock star

Adrian Messenger—young CEO of high-tech startup

George-776—Adrian's creation assistant

Jaden Larkin—young teacher and freelance author

Jaina Baskin—punk rich kid

Annette Bushkov—middle-aged woman and member of a religious cult

Andy Garza—Dahlia's soon to be ex-boyfriend

Anton Noidtal—man of many interests and founder of Child Champs

On Mars

Skyler Abercromby and Phil-422—administrators of Mars when colonists arrive

Kim ManDoo, Yang ZeDong—colonists who come with the Chinese colony clubs

NIMBY: Not in Mars' Backyard!

With months of work, the human delegation lead by Carl Earsly had worked their way through to a meeting with the human head of the Space Agency, and now, finally, to a meeting with the creation-side director, Jim-426—the decision maker on this project.

"My goodness, you humans are persistent," it said.

"We've been on this world a long time," Earsly responded patiently.

"But now you humans have handed over many of the material aspects of making a living here on Earth to us creations, and that's why you're here." The creation gave a reasonable imitation of a human sigh, then continued, "You want a human colony on Mars, and I'm afraid we still can't allocate resource to that project. I'm sorry."

"We are here to change your mind on that."

"It will be very difficult, Mr. Earsly. There are many reasons why a Mars colony is still not feasible."

"We of this delegation don't see why we still have a problem, Jim. As of this year, the Space Agency is now accepting tourist flights to Mars, and you've built a billion dollar series of resort complexes there to receive them. What's the difference between tourists and colonists?"

"Age, Mr. Earsly," Jim-426 said confidently. "The tourists are all humans of full maturity, over 30 years old. They have lived through childhood, teenagehood, and their crazy twenties. They are ready to accept more responsibility, and with that they can take more risk. We will take fully mature humans to Mars, not children."

"Not children?"

"A core part of the creation charter is to 'Think of the Children', Mr. Earsly. I'm sure you're quite aware of that. That means we will make every effort to insure that every human child conceived becomes a mature adult, an adult of age thirty, and we will make every effort to make sure that a mature adult gets all the material support he or she needs to live a healthy and happy life. The mature adult can take some risks that a child cannot, one being space tourism."

"But building colonies on Mars has always been part of the human dream."

"Hardly always, Mr. Earsly! Only for the last two hundred years or so. It was not until scientists and science fiction readers really began to believe that Earth and planets were similar in their structure that you humans could dream of colonizing Mars. Your species existed tens of thousands of years with no such dream."

Earsly ignored his reply and continued, "And what about Neolithic Parks?"

Jim-426 gave the creation equivalent of a frown. "The Neolithic Parks have always been a problem for us creations. They are so against the Charter! Children die there, many of them! And neither they nor mature adults get full material support. Yes, we would fix that all in an instant! We would!... But they are specifically outside our charter."

"What if you could get rid of them, Jim?"

"Jim-426, if you don't mind. There are so many Jim creations in this organization."

He continued, "Integrating them—not 'getting rid of them', if you don't mind—would be nice, but they are an insurance policy. We—humans and creations—keep them because they are insurance against humans going extinct should there be a civilization-collapsing catastrophe here on Earth. Only those who are currently thriving in Stone Age conditions will have the genes and knowledge to keep thriving should all the earth suddenly revert to Stone Age conditions again.

"We creations see the Neolithic Parks as an expensive program, mostly because of all the suffering those humans must feel, but all insurance policies seem expensive until their catastrophe hits."

Earsly persisted, "So, I ask again: What if you could get rid of them?"

Jim-426 managed to look confused. "I don't know what you're leading up to, Mr. Earsly?"

"A clause in the Neolithic Park charter states that if humans are established in self-sufficient colonies on many other worlds, then the parks no longer need to exist on Earth."

Jim-426 looked cross-eyed for a moment as he did some remote document searching. When his attention came back to the room, he smiled. "You and your delegation may be on to something, Mr. Earsly. I thank you for bringing this to my attention."

The delegation filed out. One quiet member of that delegation was Anton Noidtal, a graduate student who was an Earsly protégé and president of the Mars Colonizing Club at his university. Ten years from now, he will found Child Champs, and ten years after that, Child Champs will have a reputation as one of the top places in New York City to learn about child bearing and child raising.

And Dahlia Rose will be one of his top teachers there.

BOOK ONE:

LIGHT SIDE STORIES

Chapter One

Welcome to Child Champs

Welcome to Child Champs. I'm Dahlia Rose, I teach here.

Yes, this classroom around me is spartanly furnished, but Child Champs isn't cheap—our reputation is that of being one of the best places to learn about child-raising in the city.

The students come in one by one. This is the first day of class, and there is some first day confusion, but not much because Child Champs has only eight classrooms, and each of these could squeeze in twelve people each at most. Today's class starts at 8PM, and I'm scheduled to have seven students.

This class is our basic and most popular. We teachers have nicknamed it Rugrat 101, but we are careful not to use that name around students or managers. For them it is Parenting Fundamentals for the PAT—the PAT class for short. PAT is Parent Achievement Test. You take the PAT to determine your ranking in all things related to child raising. This ranges from employment by others to what to do when you receive your "bundle of joy" from a government-sponsored baby development lab. The higher your score, the more choices you have in which baby will become yours and where you get to raise it. Think SAT and college choice and you're not far off the mark.

I watch the students come in. Each class is different because a lot of different kinds of people want to raise children. Our classes meet in person once a week. This adds a lot to the cost of the class. We have to have rooms and teachers—like me—and the prospective parents have to do some traveling. But as our founder, Anton Noidtal, puts it, "Raising children isn't a job, it's an adventure!" We charge more than the purely online programs, but our students get more, too, and that's why we consider ourselves the best the city has to offer.

The students have different backgrounds. We will all find out more when we do the introductions.

It's five minutes before class. I hear some yakking outside the classroom door, a "bye", and in comes a young woman with an old Raspberry of some sort. She's smallish, slim, Asian-looking with long black hair, and wearing jeans and a T-shirt with a slogan on it—"Don't Drink and Derive" plastered over some math formulas. Cute! The T-shirt and jeans look good on her, but it's not this year's fashion. She's probably an immigrant. She sees the sign in the classroom saying, "Please turn off devices that may interrupt your concentrating on the class." and reaches up to switch something on the unit. Ancient, which means she is poor, which means she is in class to make money—she will probably become some couple's nanny or surrogate mother. She may not know much to start with, but she's early, which means she's likely to work hard at the class. I like that kind of student.

First Class

"Hi there, and welcome to the class," I say after my new student turns off her Raspberry.

She is a bit shy, and when she speaks I understand why: She is definitely an immigrant, and she's still working on her English, too. English and kids—she's going to be a busy, busy woman for the next few years! But it's a common combination.

Next to come in is a couple. They are older—the man has let his hair gray, the woman has not. They seem to be on good terms with each other. They see the sign about turning off phones and do something internal. Their equipment and clothing are up to date. They are likely into baby raising because they think it's now the right time in their lives.

"Hi there!" I say. "My goodness, it's stormy tonight!" I encourage small talk between students before class. By the end of the course, we should all know each other well. If we don't, then coming to a face-to-face class like this has been a waste of money for the students. They should have stuck with online courses.

Next comes a rush of students. It is close to class starting time. A punk-looking teenage girl, a nice-but-not-noticeable man, and a no-nonsense businessman type come in. The businessman is yakking to someone as he comes in, looks around, sees the sign, and walks out to finish his talking. While he is talking outside, a striking woman in expensive clothes and sunglasses slides by him and walks in. I'd heard rumors, and they look to be true! She takes off her sunglasses and she is Rubyzin, the pop singer with a couple of platinum albums! Ummm, I can feel my insides thrill with fan awe! I like her stuff!

Then there is a surprise. The night manager stands at the door and motions for me to come out. I do. The look on his face is serious as he says, "I apologize for this short notice, but I have one more student I'd like to put in your class." He motions. She is standing at the end of the hall. She's a woman in a full length flowing dress and wearing a scarf—clearly a member of some conservative religious group. We don't get that kind often here because they usually handle all their making and raising within their own group, so there's a story here. Maybe we will hear it, maybe not.

"Sure," I say. I'm an open-minded type. He motions and she walks up and by us quietly to take her place in the classroom.

"Thanks," says the manager, looking relieved, and he heads off. I head into the classroom. The man finishes his phone talking and walks in behind me. We are all there—time for class to begin!

"Welcome to the Child Champs Parenting Fundamentals for the PAT class," I say. "I'm Dahlia Rose, your facilitator.

"One of the benefits of a Child Champs class is the help you'll get from your fellow students, and me, so let's start by getting to know each other a little.

"I'm 38 years old, and I'm a baby labs child myself. My day job is event coordinator at DeMuzzy High Fashion. I got a 92nd percentile on the PAT's last year. And yes, I get some spam from baby labs. I don't have a baby yet because I'm still looking for my Mr. Right, but I do plan on raising my children while I'm young. I'm still close with my family, and that's a little about me."

I motion to the student on my right. It's the immigrant girl with the Raspberry. "Hi... I'm Miranda An. I'm from Laos. It's between China, Vietnam, and Thailand. My father is still there, but my mother, sister, and I have come to the US. I work at Hamburger Heaven, and I want to move from working there into child raising as soon as I can."

"Welcome to the class," I say with a smile, and I motion to the next student—students actually—this is the man and woman who are clearly paired up in some way. I look at them more closely now. They are old, but they are fighting it. Their skin is a bit thin and leathery, which says lots of outdoor or tanning salon time in the past. There is leather in their skin, but not many wrinkles, which says both have spent time and money on looking younger. Fifty years ago that look would have screamed Botox, but nowadays there are a lot of things that work better than Botox, but they aren't cheap.

"We're Janet and Ben Hosker," says Ben in a relaxed way. "We are semi-retired now. We have seen a lot, and now it's time to tell some children about what we've seen."

That was it. Short and sweet. It caught me off guard. "I'm sure we'll hear a lot more as we all get better acquainted," I say and point to the next student.

The next student is Rubyzin. She is sitting at the far end of the table. As I point to her, she looks around in a friendly, peer-to-peer way.

There is directness, not drama in her talking, "Hi, I'm Rubyzin, and it's a pleasure to meet all of you. I'm in the entertainment business. I sing for a living, but I take the business part of my business seriously, too. I'm looking forward to getting to know all of you better."

I hope she is sincere about the last part. This is one of the perks of teaching at Child Champs. It's the best in the city, so the city's best often show up here. Knowing a popular star is going to look good on my resume.

"And you're planning on raising a child because...," I prompt her to continue.

She looks at me a moment before replying. "Because now is the right time." She says it as if this were a terribly obvious answer. She's giving us the no-answer answer. We'll find out more with time. I motion to the student sitting next to her. It's the businessman who was yakking in the hall.

The man starts in a friendly, but direct way, "Hi everyone. I'm Adrian Messenger, CEO of Gene Editors, Inc. We make some of the machines that are used to make the babies. Like Rubyzin, I'm here because now is the right time."

Hmmm, nice. The handsome president of a high tech startup. He's a hot prospect, if he's not already attached. I look discreetly, and he's not wearing a ring. I really, really, really want to ask, "Are you in play?" but I don't. But at some point, I will! Instead, I motion to the next student.

The next student is the nondescript man. He continues his nondescriptness by acting shy and starting his introduction slowly. "... Hi everyone, I'm Jaden Larkin. I teach at Obama Middle School for my day job, and I moonlight at writing entertainment scripts—commercials, videos, music videos—things like that. I haven't had my big break yet, but that will come."

"Do you do song writing?" asks Rubyzin.

"... Why yes, a little," he says.

"Didn't you do the song on the Peach car commercial? That's nice work."

Jaden's smile beams across the room. "Why thank you, Ruby. May I call you that?" Clearly, she has made his day, and I'm impressed, too. Ruby is no slouch at her work if she's up on that kind of industry trivia.

Jaden continues, "To finish, I'm planning on raising a child to supplement my income. Freelance entertainment writing is very feast or famine."

I motion to the next student. She's wearing a Neopunk outfit, including the weird-colored hair, inch-thick makeup, and piercings, and she's been steadily chewing a piece of gum while the others were talking.

"Hi all," she waves, "I'm... a... kinda, like, here to learn about kids. I dropped out of City Tech and my... um... folks really want me to get some kind of good work. They are paying me to come here… I mean, paying *for* me to come here. I think raising kids is, like, really important for our society. If we don't raise them well, we'll get lots of punks and criminals on the streets.… That's all."

"And your name?" I ask. I hope it doesn't show, but I think this punky girl is likely to be the class pill—the one that is hard to take. She sounds like a just-out-of-high-school class loser with rich parents. I hope, I really hope, I'm wrong. God! I hate those types with a passion!

"Jaina Baskin," she says.

"Anything to do with Baskin-Robbins?" I ask. I'm trying to make a joke.

"I'm a great-something-grandchild of Burt Baskin," she replies, as if she is somewhat embarrassed by the answer. I know I am! I was expecting a laugh and "No Way!" answer. Uh-oh, now I have to find out if I'm dealing with an old-money spoiled brat or a poor, ignorant punk from a no-inheritance side of the family who is as loser as she looks to be. I will find that out later.

I motion to the final student. She's the quiet one in the long dress and scarf. She was quiet and demure coming in, but now she speaks with authority, "I'm Annette Bushkov. I'm part of the Reaching for Paradise commune. I'm here because I'm infertile, but my husband and I still want to do our part in bringing forth the next generation." And she's finished. The story smells like limburger in a perfume factory: Incurable infertility is rare these days, and these closed-commune types usually handle this kind of domestic problem among themselves, so we're going to find out a lot more later, I'm sure of that!

"OK, now that we've all been introduced, let's talk about what the class will be about," I begin my spiel.

To start the class, I hand around a flyer.

The Ad

Our babies are 98% Einstein! You're looking for the best baby to raise, and our babies are the best. We have spared no expense to prepare the best gene package you can get for the money, and our incubators are state of the art. They will prepare you a cuddly bundle of love that has everything it needs to grow into a world shaker!

It's on glossy paper, and five years ago it was passed out in the local shopping malls once a week.

I pass the ad around to the class.

"OK," I ask the students, "what's wrong with this ad? How is it misleading?"

Ben Hosker snorts a laugh. "Even chimpanzees have 98% Einstein genes!"

"Very good," I say. "Advertisers for baby labs are no more scrupulous than those for any other consumer product. If an ad like this sells a baby, they win. These days some advertising standards have been agreed upon by the baby labs, so this ad no longer appears. Still, you need to know your product basics if you are going to make an intelligent choice. So understanding child making and child raising basics is half of this class. The other half, and closely related, is helping you do well on the PAT test."

Dahlia's Lesson

Lesson One—PAT's: What's at Stake?

From human prehistory up until the early 21st century, child rearing started when a man and a woman formed a family unit through a marriage of some kind. It continued when they made love with each other—in other words, the man and the woman of the marriage provided the genetic material for the child, and providing that material was the signal to start the child rearing process. After the child was born they personally did most of the things involved with child rearing.

This wasn't the only way to make and raise children, as evidenced by the huge interest in "drama" in human story telling about families—stories about adoption, nannies, and infidelity—but it was a common way the world over. These days this method is still practiced by rural families in poor nations, some fundamentalist religious groups, and those living in Neolithic Parks.

One of the new challenges that humans face in this 22nd century of ours is that not enough people want to raise families in this traditional way. In the first decades of the 21st century, most humans had become urban people. Since most urban people have so many other things to do, family raising has been pushed out of their lives. This phenomenon—that prosperous city people don't have enough children to sustain the population—was noted as early as the nineteenth century by British demographers. But it didn't matter until the 21st century because before then most humans lived on the farm. Around 2008 the split was even, and the percentage of city dwellers has been steadily rising ever since.

These days a majority of rural people still raise their own children, but these days there aren't a lot of rural people. They are only ten percent of the population. The only urban people who consistently raise more children than the replacement level are those religious groups which take the "be fruitful and multiply" commandments seriously.

So two trends are reshaping the modern baby making scene. One is the population is declining, which means governments are now sponsoring child making and raising in various ways. The other is the tools available to make and raise children are proliferating, and just like since prehistory, everyone who gets involved in raising a child wants the best for that child. The result is today we have baby-making laboratories to make the needed babies and "baby villages" as places to raise them.

The "baby labs" gather the best of eggs and sperm, add everything modern science can add in the way of diagnostics and gene enhancements, go through a couple more steps that people don't like to talk about, and produce the best babies, ready to be raised by loving parents.

Baby labs can make babies and mature them into fetuses ready to be born, but they can't grow them from toddlers into adult humans ready for modern life—that growing up part still takes people willing to spend lots of time and attention on youngsters.

There are many ways to do baby raising. Some are quick and simple; some are long, elaborate, and expensive. There are new ways, and there are old ways. There are dozens of magazines and web sites devoted to discussions of what makes good babies and what makes babies grow up into good adults. In short, there are "Ferrari babies" that people would give their eye teeth to raise, "Ford babies" that need to be raised just to keep humanity going, and dozens of kinds in between. And there are dozens of kinds of places where babies can be raised. Some are luxury, some are commodity, and many are in between. The PAT's are an important part of the process that decides who raises what, and where.

The PAT is a standardized test that measures a person's parenting aptitude. When a person decides they want to take a baby from a baby lab and raise it, and have the government contribute in various ways to their raising efforts, part of their qualifying dossier is their PAT test. The two other main considerations are their financial condition and their community report -- the recommends from their friends, neighbors, and coworkers.

Those three—PAT's, finances, and recommends—are the heart of the parent selecting process used by the baby labs, the baby villages, and the government. Throughout this course we will be working on ways you can raise your standing when you're being considered for baby making and child raising programs and support.

—— End of Lesson ——

As soon as the class ends, the students gather their stuff and walk out. In the hall most start their "zombie act"—they start phone calling, text messaging, and whatever. The only problem with that is that the hall becomes barely navigable when so many distracted callers fill it up.

My students get a ten minute lead on me in getting hooked back into "real life" because I have paperwork to fill out at the end of class. I get to report to management on who was here and what we covered in the various texts, power points, and videos—Anton Noidtal, the boss, is very picky about making sure the students get value added when they have a class here.

As I am finishing up, I get an unexpected visitor: Anton himself! My first thought is, "Uh-oh, what have I done?" But he doesn't look angry and when he speaks, it is kindly and supportive.

"I want to thank you for taking Annette Bushkov into your class."

"My pleasure," I say.

"She is an experiment—on the part of her group and Child Champs. Cult groups such as hers could become an interesting niche market for child raising. They raise a lot of kids, you know.

"If anything unusual pops up, please let me know." He smiles again warmly and heads off.

Ten minutes later, I walk into the main lobby and do my zombie act—I link back into real life, too. Once I have all the crises-of-the-hour covered, I head for home.

Breaking Up

While heading home, I handle the real crisis—the one that has been brewing for some time. For some reason, I like to do my "messy" calls while I'm in my car and the car is driving. I guess looking at the scenery going by soothes me from the people problems I face while making a messy call.

This messy problem is that I've decided to break up with Andy—Andy Garza. He's been nice, and he seems to like me a lot, but I just don't think he's enough of a provider. I'm ready to start "pollinating for effect", but he's still in gather-life-experiences mode. He says he's in love, and I believe that. I just don't believe he's ready to get into the child raising part of a relationship, and that's what I need right now—someone to help on the child raising.

I dial him up and he's in. We small talk for a bit, and then I drop the bomb. "Andy, we need to slip our relationship back to just-friends mode."

There is silence on the other end for a while. "Have you started taking pills?"

The pills are "forget him" pills. They help a girl, or a guy, get over a relationship that's gone sour. The pills adjust the "raging hormones of youth" brain chemistry to help the brain reprogram the notion that a girl's object of affection isn't really the center of the known universe—he's just another man. An important secondary effect is that a woman doesn't have a big problem with being "on the rebound" after she breaks up—ready to hook up with the next testosterone producer who asks her. Boys have their own set of pills to help them with heartbreak and rage/revenge/ depression thinking.

"Not yet," I say. If I had said yes, Andy probably would just say, "OK, good bye and good luck," and that would be it. The pills cut down interest pretty quickly, and unless you like dating cold fish, you're not going to like dating someone who's taking "forget him" pills for you. I could have lied and said yes, but I didn't, so I hear…

"Want to get together for dinner and a last kiss?" He's nice, and I really do like him, so I say yes, and we set a date. When the call ends, I'm relieved. This breakup looks like it's going to go smoothly. We'll have our last kiss, and then both start on pills, and we'll be just friends for as long as our interests are mutual. My grandmother doesn't believe that this can happen, but these days it's true.

A few minutes later he calls back, "I just had a thought. Want to do this last kiss at the top of Butterfield Canyon… at sunset?"

There are some implications to that setting that send tingles to my nipples. "Umm, we can do that," I say, "but keep in mind: this is a last kiss date."

"I will, I will," he says.

Last kiss dates can sometimes be very memorable. This may be one of those times.

Chapter Two

Oh, Give Me One Last Kiss

The night for the last kiss date comes. Andy picks me up at work. That's fine because I'm not going to have to dress special for this. The furnishings at the Shangri-La Love Motel will take care of that.

Our first stop is for pizza. It's fast, simple, and we both like it that way. Being fast, it leaves us all the more time to enjoy the motel.

We don't waste time. We head there next. It's costing us a bundle, so even though it's still dinner time, we check in and head up to start our festivities.

The Shangri-La is equipped with state-of-the-art pleasure avatars. The furnishings can both simulate and avatar—sometimes we are in virtual space-powering bits, sometimes we are in real space-powering physical bodies, avatars.

Some people like to get drunk or high before taking their pleasure, but Andy and I like our pleasure straight. It's part of why we get along so well. We suit up and get started.

The first stop is a simulation. We head for a 1940s-era nightclub ballroom with a big band and do some social dancing. Andy and I both took dancing lessons as we grew up, so we can do the basic moves, and we're not too clumsy. But in v-space like this, we can do even more. We can get pretty good! With the sim helping us with coordination feedback, we work up to some Fred Astaire-Ginger Rogers stuff, and the band starts playing just for us. After a finale dance, we bow to all, head off stage, and move on to...

A ballet performance. We're in a dancing mood, so we up the ante a bit. Neither of us do ballet in real life, so we just do a couple of basic routines out of Nutcracker Suite and accept the sim coordination and the sim audience applause. And this time, we move on to something completely different...

Andy has had fun and he's been patient, but now he wants to get out of this "chick stuff", so next we move into one of his favorites. He's going to drive me up Butterfield Canyon in Utah. We will be powering real world avatars in this adventure. The road winds up a canyon in the Rocky Mountains and leads to a high mountain pass that overlooks a huge open-pit mine with the whole of Salt Lake City sprawling behind it. The view is something, and the drive is exciting, too.

We pop out in a 4x4 pickup that's in the parking lot. Andy is in the driver's seat. He's being real Western Country on this adventure. I indulge by wearing a peasant blouse, jeans, cowboy boots, and a long blond braid. I'm next to him, and I cuddle up with him. Before he starts the engine, he puts his arm around my shoulder for a moment, then slides it down under my peasant blouse and back up to my breast. I don't have a bra on. He smiles at me and kisses me. I kiss him back. Before we half think about it, it's liplock time! Oh yeah!

When we come up for air, he starts the engine. I tell him, "Keep your hands on the wheel now, cowboy." I say it in a teasy way, but in truth, he really has to!

On the way up, I split my time between watching scenery, getting warmed up by Andy's touching, and rubbing his leg in a really nice way. He would do the same, but he's set this situation so the avatar is actually doing the driving and he's actually controlling the avatar.

Doing the driving! Pfft! It's macho bullshit, and sure enough, we pay! There's a snowbank across the road partway up. We are following a big flatbed truck, and it grinds its way through it, leaving foot-deep ruts. We follow and get stuck! Fortunately, Andy has the presence to honk the horn, and the truck stops to help us.

These are locals, and while I get behind the wheel, their and Andy's strong backs push us back out downhill. Whew!

Then the chief local comes over and takes a quick glance at our instrument panel. He points while he says, "You may want to take your snowbanks in four wheel drive, son."

Then he asks, "Where ya from, anyway?" in a neighborly way. I'm relieved—this could have gone a lot worse. We could have been marooned up here for an hour while someone brought up a tow truck, and these locals could have made serious mockery of us in our avatar sets.

"New York City," explains Andy, "but my grandfather lived out here in Herriman. That's how I found out about this place."

The local agrees. He looks at the two of us and says, "You'll get a fine view up there. I proposed to my wife up there… That's been a while now." He laughs. "Have a good time." He may be reading us wrong, but not that wrong. We smile at each other, and thank him again.

Andy engages the four wheel drive, and as the locals watch, we grind through the snowbank as smoothly as the big truck did. Everyone cheers, and we all get back underway again.

We follow them only a few more minutes, then they take a different fork and head down Middle Canyon, according to the sign. They wave and we wave, and off we go headed for the overlook.

By the time we get to the overlook, we are both feeling real warm and fuzzy again. He parks. It's close to sunset. The view is stunning. I get out and walk around to take one last look at the scenery while I wait to get "jumped" by Andy. I don't have to wait long.

He comes up behind me and rubs my arms and breasts a bit, then, with a fast move, he pins my arms behind me with one hand and puts his other hand over my face.

I am in his control. I arch my back a bit and look up. He kisses my neck, then moves his hand from my face to the back of my head and controls my head with my braid. I'm loving it. I respond to his every push and tug.

He leads me back to the truck. The tailgate is down, and there is a mattress in the back to cover the pickup bed. He flops me face first on the mattress. My feet are on the ground; my tummy and face are on the mattress. He lets go of my arms, but I hold them behind me. I know what comes next.

From somewhere Andy pulls out a rope and holds it over my back so that some of the loops drag over my arms and back. He does this for about thirty seconds, and it is such a turn-on! Then I feel the coils of rope start looping around my elbows and wrists. I'm a cowgirl and I'm being tied up!

We've done this a few times now, so he ties me well. I'm helpless. I'm his! And I'm really, really happy about being this way. This is one of the things I really like about Andy. I'll miss it...

The moon rises over the mountains across the valley as we rest peacefully on the mattress. Andy gets up to stretch his legs and wanders over to the overlook and starts watching the mining machinery at work. We are so far away that you have to listen hard to hear the machinery, but it's all so big, you have no trouble seeing it! When it's clear he's happy there, I get up, join him, and slip under his arm.

"We should come back some time and operate those machines. That would be a blast." He says that just as someone below sets off a dynamite charge and part of a cliff side tumbles down. We both giggle at that.

"Weren't you just complaining about doing chick stuff?" I rub his chest and give him a quick kiss. He laughs and smiles back, "OK. That'll be a boys' night out."

For our finale episode, we go real traditional. We go to Pandora. Yeah, the setting is inspired by that hundred-year-old movie: Jungle planet with floating mountains where you fly around. It may be a hundred years old, but it's still hard to beat! We are far from alone on this sim, there are hundreds of others out. But it's a big comfortable place. We fly, cavort, and finally settle down, exhausted, in a fairyland glen. We were planning on more cavorting, but just getting cuddly and sleepy feels sooo good!

... We wake up the next morning back in the Shangri-La room in the real world.

(Oh, and just so you know, when we left the avatars up on the Butterfield Canyon overlook, some creations took control and drove them back. These days, getting there is all the fun, and creations worry about getting stuff back.)

Over breakfast we talk about the breakup. He agrees he's not ready for child raising. He asks if I'm sure I am, and I tell him, "Yes, I'm really sure."

That decided, we spend the rest of breakfast calling people and catching up on news for the day. It's a workday, so we both have lots to do.

That day, I start on my pills, and by week's end my time with Andy will be many warm, delicious memories, but he will not be someone I still feel hot for. If he takes pills—and I presume he will—the feeling will be mutual.

This is some of the new biotechnology at its nicest. In the old movies, the girl's plea to "let's just be friends" was a silly one—neither could really think that way once the hormones heated up. Nowadays it's quite common, and that chunk of plot building looks as silly as the plot device in even older movies where a man murders his wife because she won't divorce him. These particular pills are part chemistry and part nanobot—bacteria-sized machines. These bots will be floating in my gut and my bloodstream. I've got a bunch in me already helping with digestion and just generally keeping me healthy.

For Andy and me, it's time to get on with life, and pills will help us do that quickly and painlessly.

Adrian's Gene Editors Video

It's time for our second class.

Adrian comes in and announces, "Who wants to see the latest Gene Editors promo video. It stars… me!"

We all laugh and clap and say, "Sure."

Adrian pops us the URL and we sit back.

Adrian is sitting in an office looking well-groomed and executive-like. He is smooth and comfortable when he says, "Welcome to Gene Editors. I'm Adrian Messenger, CEO, and I'd like to tell you about our latest product.

"At Gene Editors, we are developing the tools that advance the genetics revolution. We don't make the breakthroughs—we provide the tools that let others make breakthroughs. We allow thousands of genetics geniuses to express themselves quicker, faster, and cheaper. If we were in the Old West at the Gold Rush, we would be providing shovels to the prospectors.

"What I will tell you about today is our latest shovel." Adrian pulls a real shovel from behind his desk. "Whoops, not this kind!" he grins. The view changes to a swirl of graphics mixed with shots of engineers in a lab "slaving over hot monitors" while Adrian says, "The new tool suite offered by Gene Editors is transforming genetic engineering into word processing.

"Genes tell a story by producing proteins and folding them up into useful patterns. With Gene Editors "Plot Device" tools, a genetic engineer can access the basic grammar of DNA and understand the first level implications of his or her changes. Gene Editors Plot Device tools will point out what other protein synthesis is directly affected by changes the editor is making.

"This ability will speed up the development of useful enzymes in bacterial synthesis, make the development of antibiotics a process that takes hours, not weeks, and widen the scope of biomaterials manufacturing.

"And we provide an open source library so editors can build on the work of other editors."

The scene switches to a wholesome family scene with kids playing in the park. "Our lives—all our lives—are going to become a whole lot better thanks to Gene Editors products."

The video finishes and we applaud again.

"Congratulations," says Ben. "So, are sales going well?"

"This is something we won't release for another six weeks, but sales of our existing products are doing well. We've been able to report better-than-projected results to our investors."

"Very impressive for a startup," comments Ben.

"Thanks, Ben. Yeah, this phase of Gene Editors has been quite gratifying. Frankly, we are getting good results sooner than I expected. People are getting the idea really quickly."

"Your equating gene editing and word processing makes it sound like something even I could master," I laugh.

"Well... should we see what we can get you creating?" he grins back.

"We should... but not right now. It's time for class. Let's all take a look at our next lesson."

Dahlia's Lesson

Lesson Two—Baby Making Overview

Two hundred years ago, there was only one way to make a baby. The only variation possible was who to make a baby with. A hundred years ago, medical technology had advanced enough that the first primitive variations from the traditional method became possible. Today, we have dozens of ways to make babies, and the popular ones each have their strengths and weaknesses.

The variations center around five things:

Who produces the sperm and who produces the egg

Who modifies the DNA and other heredity carriers in the sperm and the egg

Where is the zygote developed into a fetus

Where is the fetus developed into a ready-to-be-born child

What environment is this person-to-be adapted for?

After the child is born, a whole new collection of choices present themselves, centering on how to raise a child from newborn to grade school age. And after that come the choices on how to handle grade schoolers, and so on.

What this series of lessons will talk about is how to acquire a baby—how all of the above mix with current commercial, government, and legal realities to produce your current baby-acquiring choices.

—— End of Lesson ——

Chapter Three

Miranda's New Job

By the third class, we are getting pretty familiar with each other. And today turns out to be a pretty special one for both Miranda and Jaden.

Miranda comes to class beaming, just beaming.

"Good news?" asks Jaden.

"Very good," she replies. "I got job as an assistant therapist at the Nomad Relief Center in Astoria."

"Congratulations," says Jaden in a neutral way. And, in truth, it didn't sound like much to me, either. These days there is a new twist on that old saying, "If you can't do, teach." The new twist is "If you can't teach, be a therapist."

"It's so good because my family and I are now in system," she says. "We now all have insurance. And my mother now has free membership at the community center. She has place to spend some time other than home, and she can take English classes there."

"It sounds like a nice first step," I say, and I mean that. I'd forgotten just how far the Ans had to come now that they were in the US.

"What will you do there?" asks Annette.

"Some of the nomads get pretty discouraged with their lifestyle. When they do, some of them go overboard and get into self-destructive behavior. That gets expensive for them and the community."

"I'll say!" grunts Adrian.

"We help them transition into something more sustainable."

"What will do you do, specifically?"

"Oh, I mostly help patients get to and back from their therapy sessions. I help them be comfortable. It feels much like working in tea house in Laos. There girls help customers lose their stress. Here I do same thing... but the American way."

We all laugh at that.

"Welcome to America," adds Adrian.

Jaden's Class Act

Jaden had come into class strutting and beaming too—something good has definitely happened.

"And what's your good news?" Annette inquires.

"My students and I just won first prize in the state competition for a video we did."

We all applaud and cheer. Jaden beams even more.

"It was a science fiction short. Dinosaurs invaded the school! We had the kids running around and screaming, and we added some really neat special-effects dinosaurs chasing them around. One kid did a great job of getting eaten! We ended it with it being just a dream."

"Sounds like a classic," I say laughing.

"It was... and we even got called up on one point in it by a paleontologist geek. He pointed out that in one scene, one of the kids points at a dinosaur off screen and calls him a stegosaurus, but what we put up next was a dimetrodon. I couldn't find the steg clip, so I punted."

We all laugh at that.

"It was a lot of fun, and I got a personal congratulations from the state superintendent."

"So... are we looking at a future assistant principal?" asks Janet.

Jaden beams back, then adds, "This TMG I got is making quite a difference."

"TMG? As in "Taj Mahal Girl"? You got one of those? What kind?" asks Ruby.

"Oh, it's just a virtual one. The state started providing them to selected teachers last year. It's part of the new contract we negotiated. It's an experiment to see if we can boost productivity.

"So far, I've been pretty happy with mine. I call her Ginger. I can feel that she's given me a lot more energy. In fact, she's partly why I'm here."

"How so?" asks Ruby.

"She's making me comfortable with my nest-building instincts again," laughs Jaden.

"Sounds quite useful for this class," says Ben.

"OK, folks," I say, bringing the class to order, "let's get started on today's lesson."

Dahlia's Lesson

Lesson Three—Sperm and Egg Producers

Historically the most common sperm producer was the husband in a marriage, and the egg producer was the wife. Although even in pre-history there have been many variations on that theme—variations such as adoption, infidelity, rape, romantic encounter, and incest—nowadays there are many more choices available. Sperm banks provide numerous male donor options with the advantage of many choices, and these can be tested and rated in many categories. Egg banks offer eggs, but not with nearly the variety that are available in sperm banks.

Because they are so much harder to acquire from living, breathing females, the eggs in egg banks are mostly either clones of the best eggs from high-profile donors such as Olympic winner Brenda Bonnie or spawned in ovary banks from vat ovaries that have never experienced life in a whole human. In theory, eggs that have never experienced real life are not a problem, but… this is a topic of much discussion among child raisers these days.

How these translate into personal choices:

You as a baby raiser have three basic choices, then lots of variations on those.

1) Use your own sperm and egg. The variations then come in the form of how much inspection and modifying you want to do on your own legacy source. This can range from a little—a few choose none at all, trusting in God—to a whole lot. Most choose some modification, and how much is determined by what a person sees as cost effective and within their budget. The choices are plentiful and widely varied in terms of price, promise, what can be modified, and proven effectiveness.

2) Start with someone else's sperm or egg. Those who go this route want to buy rich and famous. As soon as you make a name for yourself, you'll start getting offers from the baby labs to become a donor. If you read any gossip news at all, you're well aware of how much the top names can make and how much they cost. And there are the soap opera-style scams where people steal germ cells in one way or another, such as the prostitutes who claim they have some of "X" or "Y"'s sperm from some "sporting" they did with them on a wild weekend.

3) Chimera germ cells. These are heavily modified mixes from many sources. They are used for growing people who will be living in specialized environments such as deep sea habitations.

I will caution you: There is a lot more promise being offered out there than tangible delivery. But baby growing is such a deeply emotional process that paying for "feel-good" sometimes seems to make sense.

One of the main functions of this class will be for us, as a group, to sort through what we find is offered and try to make a reasonable assessment—how much of an offering is real and how much is feel-good? I freely admit that even though I'm the class teacher and I scored well on the PAT, I don't have all the answers—

things change too quickly, and each of us will feel different things are important.

So we will research together, and we will make different choices. This is the nature of modern baby making.

—— End of Lesson ——

Fashion Week

As I said earlier, my day job is with DeMuzzy High Fashion. And the yearly high point of that job is Fashion Week.

Fashion Week is living hell, but I wouldn't have it any other way.

The rest of the year at DeMuzzy High Fashion is all about Fashion Week, or so it seems the closer we get to it. This is when we strut our stuff. And if we strut it well, we are busy the rest of the year filling orders. If we don't, we stare across the table at each other, sweating blood, as we prepare for next year's Fashion Week.

I've had it go both ways, and believe me, you really do want to spend the year filling orders!

The first step is researching what went well last year—which means researching what is selling well this year. This is something you have to watch constantly, and there are always surprises.

Each year, six weeks after Fashion Week ends, Mr. DeMuzzy, our head honcho, calls a meeting. The purpose of the meeting is to declare the theme for next year's Fashion Week. This is not the first meeting on this topic, it's the first of the finals—the choice gets reality-checked twice more before the final push for Fashion Week is mustered.

In the six weeks before the meeting, people are getting out of their warm-fuzzy from completing the last Fashion Week and getting their noses back to the grindstone. The grindstone in this case means figuring out what is trendy.

The creations are constantly tabulating what's selling and what's not. They do it for our stuff as well as for the rest of the industry, and they do it by channels—stores, mobiles, sales categories, by sales and specials—any way you as a human want to slice it.

We watch sales and we watch people. We each program our bots to track what celebs and other trend-setters are wearing. It's our job as humans to decide who is trend-setting. Once we do, our bots take up the spy part and keep them under surveillance.

This part used to be tons of fun for me—I was getting paid to do star-watching! But it's getting to be more and more of a chore. I've seen all this now through a couple of fashion cycles, and I admit it, I'm getting out of touch. It seems these younger generations have their taste all in their mouth! What do they see in these trashy choices they make? Was I really making the same kinds of trashy choices when I was young? (In truth, I find that hard to believe… until I take a hard, business-like look back at the fashion cycle *I* grew up in.)

These days instead of playing instinctive, I play smart: I spend my effort on carefully picking who to watch, and I'm pretty cold-blooded about it. My youngest and most enthusiastic compatriots can't understand how I can watch Virginia La Gnocchi with a yawn instead of a gasp, but I still track her closely. The ones that are a bit older figure I've sold out, but they respectfully pay attention to my choices because I seem to get good value from whatever I've sold out to.

Once the theme has been hashed out at that first theme meeting, we start mustering people, companies, and creations to support it. The good news is we did this last year and the year before and so on, so the people and creation relations and contacts are all in place. The bad news is each year is different, so there are constant changes in who we have to work with.

One constant is the question of what can we afford? The theme is always a big enough idea that it could suck down ten times our budget and look grander for each dollar spent. The hard, hard question is what is the last dollar we can spend that gets us another dollar in gross profit? That's what this first theme meeting and the reality-check meetings are all about.

When the meeting is finished, the marshalling begins. The fashion creators and designers start programming their creations—programming them in the sense of describing to them what they want. They are definitely not nerds! The creations slave over the keyboards, the designers talk and pick from projections. While they are working the designs over, I'm working over the model line-up: Who's going to be hot this year? Who's going to be the impressive fresh new face? Who are the cost-effective bargains?

The hardest part is deciding who to cut bait on and how to ease them out. Sometimes those going over the hill make it easy: If they start gaining weight, or a new career, or become part of a juicy scandal, my job gets easier. That happens sometimes... other times I just have to be harsh with them, and that's no fun. I explain that their style just isn't part of this year's theme. If they've been good to work with, I will try to kick them upstairs in some fashion—something which will give them more work to do, but less profile. I try... but if the girl has no skills but walking a runway and smiling for a camera, it's tough. And some are that way: They've dedicated their whole lives to this lifestyle, and their parents have backed them one hundred percent on that choice.

Another issue is just how artificial a girl can look and still be acceptable? Some years and themes, the girls can look as artificial as android creations and do just fine... as long as they look young, too. Other years and themes the natural look is in. Then they have to look natural... and young. Of course, natural-looking is in the eye of the beholder—I've seen as much "plastic" under the skin of some of those natural beauties as those toy Barbie dolls had in their whole bodies a hundred years ago.

Whatever... it's my job to pick and choose. Then I pick and choose the creations who will do the tending, wardrobe fitting, and cosmetics of these young beauties.

There is so much at stake here, but these really *are* young girls! They are human, young human. As Fashion Week approaches and commitments are made, it gets truly spooky how much is riding on these girls strutting their stuff in a polished and professional way. Their chaperone creations are there to keep stupid things from happening.

But some have been so bred, primped, and trained for this lifestyle by their success-driven parents that they are God-like stunning on the outside, but psycho babe-monsters on the inside, and even the best chaperone creation can't stop a catastrophe. Part of my job is keeping those out of our line-up, but it's hard because those driven parents are often quite cunning and persuasive.

< < < * > > >

We're at the meeting, and this year the grand theme is… Shit! Boys!

Not only are we going to have hot women and girls working the runway, we will have to find sweet-looking boy escorts for them! HOLY HANNA! It's been looming in the pre-meetings, and I've been voting against this from paragraph one. But fashion is fashion… sigh. I can see clearly where this theme is coming from, and it's clearly a hot trend this year.

It appears I'm going to have to do some big time selling out for Fashion Week this year!

It looks like it, but halfway through the meeting I get a reprieve—harsh reality strikes. It's not a facilities issue, it's a legal issue: If we're going to mix boys and girls backstage and onstage, we will need sex predator insurance. It doesn't take five minutes to look up the rates on that, and that idea goes out the window, fast!

After a bit more mulling, the acceptable compromise comes to life: We replace the boys with avatars built to look like sweet-boy manikins. They will be expensive, but not nearly as expensive as the insurance. The discussion now centers on what they should look like, what they should be able to do, and how to make them into quick change artists.

Whew! This is a theme I can buy into, and the rest of this theme meeting goes as smoothly as these things ever do.

Tea with Ruby

After our third class session, I get a message from Rubyzin inviting me to an afternoon face-to-face. "Let's get a bit more acquainted, if you have an hour?" says the text. We set up a time and met at the Starscents near the school.

Ruby is quite gracious. "I've checked out your resume, and I'm impressed, Dahlia. You've had a lot of experience getting things organized. I was wondering if you could help me out with a small favor?"

"I'd be happy to try," I reply.

"I've just written a new children's book and want to put some illustrations—photos actually—in it of girls wearing my Rubyzin's Fashions. Is this something your company—and you specifically—could help out with? The money I make on the book itself will go to charity."

The money from any fashion sales she would keep, of course, but this is a common marketing model these days.

The only curious part is... *she* is schmoozing *me*? It should be the other way around. She is much more of a powerhouse in entertainment and business than I am. But odd as it is, it sounds like opportunity knocking.

"Sure. I can put some time into this," I say.

"Excellent!" she says, and she sounds like she means it. "I hope this is the start of a couple of mutually beneficial projects."

We spend the rest of the hour chatting and going over preliminary details.

The project goes well. It is straightforward and there are no surprises. The book starts selling well and raises both Ruby's profile and mine. And while the shoot is happening, Ruby and I get to spend some face-to-face time together, too.

We do some workouts at the gym together. I'm mostly a naturalist. I huff and puff and do whatever my body can do unassisted—other than the nanobots, of course. Ruby is an augmenter, body plus some subtle equipment—not surprising considering dance is part of her performance. She works out with augmentation so that her dance routines get better. Compared to what dancers could do even ten years ago, she looks supernatural in ability, but quite natural while she's doing it.

In the process we become friends as well as class associates. It's a nice feeling. I like Ruby's no-nonsense attitude about getting things done. For her, and me, artistic is nice but accomplishment is nicer.

Chapter Four

Jaina Gets Accepted

Jaina comes into class bouncy, bouncy, bouncy.

"What's up?" Jaden asks.

"Umm... I got accepted to Nothgonga School of Spirituality Massage."

"How neat!"

"I think so!... But my parents aren't as excited about it." She sighs, "They wanted me to apply to Smith, Radcliffe and Wellesley."

"Heavyweight stuff."

"Yeah... They wanted that, but I wasn't getting the grades for it. Well... I wasn't on my own, but my cybertutor was making up for my human deficiencies."

"The good ones do that these days."

"Yeah, and mine is a good one... But I don't want to take credit for what it's doing."

"Why not?"

"Well... it doesn't really feel like me. I mean... I'm me."

"It does work for you, right?"

"Yeah."

"Your parents spent a gruntload of money on it, right?"

"Yeah."

"Well..."

Jaina gets red, "IT'S NOT ME."

Jaden backs off.

"Anyway. What I do at Nothgonga will be me, so I'm looking forward to that… and to doing baby stuff."

Accepting a Gift

Jaina isn't the only one with good news.

Something fun happened at our office party this week. This year I was voted Teacher of the Year, and I got a nice award handed out by Anton himself. I am in a bit of a glow as we start class.

Annette also comes in looking happy. She tells the class, "Something special is coming up next week. My husband will come for a visit. I'm hoping it will be OK if he attends a class?"

"Sure," I say, "what's special that's bringing him to the Big Apple, if I may ask?"

"We're going to be working on a… special project," she says with a big, wonderful grin on her face. "I've been doing some medical research here, and getting some treatment at the fertility clinic." She grins some more.

"Really! That sounds wonderful!"

"Our prophet and leaders have agreed that being fruitful can be as important as being human-sufficient, so they are letting me and Don try some advanced medicine."

"It doesn't sound too advanced to me," says Jaina.

"It may not be to you, Jaina, but our group tries hard to be human-sufficient. We try to do as much as we can as humans first, and only then call in creation help. God gave us bodies to use. That means we do as much as we can with medicines we can make and procedures we can carry out at the colony. We are not Neolithic Parkers, but trying what I'm going to try now has taken a lot of convincing."

"Well… part of it sounds pretty down-home," she says.

Annette pauses for a moment at that, then laughs, "Yeah, that part is. The part that is new for us is getting my womb rejuvenated and scheduling my fertility. Don is skeptical, but he says he's quite willing to help out on the down-home part, as Jaina calls it, and isn't going to mind seeing some sights while we do."

We all laugh at that and wish Annette good luck.

Dahlia's Lesson

Lesson Four—Heredity (DNA) Modifiers

Egg and sperm DNA and other genetic factors can be scientifically modified. DNA in particular can be edited. This brings enormous power, but also brings surprises, as Adrian has noted. The people who do the modifying say it's so much like editing a long novel with a complex storyline that it's spooky. And like storybook editing, there's a lot of art in the process—changes in one place can produce unexpected changes in what develops in other places on the chain.

One result is there is a whole range of skills in modifying. There are a whole lot of people who have the skill to handle simple changes such as modifying eye color and restoring vitamin C metabolism to liver cells. And there are a few artists who can handle complex changes such as skin pigmentation and hair texture, and, sadly, plenty of charlatans who claim they can create geniuses, super models, superstars, and born leaders. There is also a wide range in the prices people in this business charge.

We will discuss what's currently possible, probable, and what are reasonable costs.

How these translate into personal choices:

This is the most complex issue in baby making. This is where the art flourishes. Once again, our choices range from do nothing to "How much can you afford?" There is a whole lot of unknown in this process, but what the known can accomplish is truly spectacular.

What we can do well is check for simple gene mutations that predispose to physical weaknesses such as some cancer susceptibilities and congenital birth defects. What we can't do well is get your sons laid while they are teenagers and your daughters married to doctors. That requires subtleties that are well beyond our current understanding. But that doesn't mean there aren't charlatans out there implying that they can.

Over the course of this term, and as a social network after, we will discuss what is currently being offered and what is likely to be both real and cost effective.

—— End of Lesson ——

Ruby at Madison Square Garden

"Hot news! I'm doing a gig at MSG, and I have tickets for you!
—Ruby"

This is hot news! I get details a bit later, and it's all you could hope for! She will be one of the headline acts for the "Woodstock in the Big Apple" celebration. This is a three day long event at the Garden and the opening highlight of the summer season. And this is the newly-built Ultra New Madison Square Garden—opened just two years ago.

The building is spectacular. It is located where the Liberty State Park used to be, not far from Ellis Island and the Statue of Liberty. It was designed to wow those who think the Sydney Opera House and Shanghai Buttercup Dome are impressive buildings.

This UNMSG was three years in construction, and while that was going on, there was a lot of grumbling that it was a boondoggle that was a waste of city money. But for the last year, it has routinely sold out its 500,000 indoor seating capacity at various mega-events, so that grumbling has died down.

That old grumbling has been replaced by new grumbling about congestion getting to and from the place, huge crowds, huge prices, and online scalpers getting huge profits. Personally, I think these current complaints are valid. These designers knew what they were getting into, and they couldn't do better crowd control?

The politicians and human designers have ducked, so the creations who did the design and construction legwork have responded that they did the best they could given the constraints put on them by human-designer imaginations, human political meddling, ancient human-designed building regulations, and the strength of materials—i.e., the real world.

In truth, these are the kinds of complaints that building designers like to have. It means the profits are being raked in. And, in truth, it seems like people don't really mind being treated like cattle when they come to an event such as this kind of place hosts.

And the crazy could be a lot worse. Pamplona still runs bulls! And the casualty count has gone up, not down! Burning Man out in Nevada has gone totally weird. They outlawed the main festival there years ago, but it has been replaced with more than a dozen "flash events" that spring up all up and down the east side of the Sierra range. People gather, get totally machoed out—often with the help of Android Age drugs and creation stimulators—then wander around in the desert claiming they are experiencing new realities and insights into the fate of man. The casualty count there isn't talked about much, but I've heard some strange, strange stories.

Humans can be weird, but then that weirdness is at the heart of my business.

This particular event would be, of course, a three day celebration. The highlight, on the third day, will be a spectacular indoor rainstorm over the central arena. As that is in progress, people can go down to the central arena, get naked, and go dancing around in the specially prepared mud that will be there as they listen to the final day's performances. Nostalgia can get super silly, but it was anticipated that about ten thousand people would pay extra for that privilege.

I know all this because we at DeMuzzy are planning to participate... in some fashion, pardon the pun. But exactly how to strut our stuff in the middle of a mud pile filled with naked dancing people has been a big, big challenge. When we first heard about this, we laughed our asses off. Since then, the panic—er, challenge—has been faced more squarely. This is when human imagination is truly, truly called for.

What we finally came up with, and I think it was inspired, was to have the food and rec-drug vendors—who would be plying that naked, muddy crowd—dressed by DeMuzzy. We'd dress them in bold, good-looking Teflon. Teflon so that they could clean up with a few seconds of hosing down, or rain, and keep plying the crowd. That decided, the remaining effort went into designing something bold, cleanable, and brand-recognizable—to a dance- and drug-crazed crowd—nothing special there.

So when I got that message from Ruby, it was super fun to hear that she would be participating as well, and that I might get a seat far, far away from that mud pile!

< < < * > > >

The two days before the first day of the show I was in backwoods New Jersey somewhere on a farm—a for-real historical farm, one with a fresh-plowed field. I was making sure the creations had everything mustered for the girls. They were on this farm practicing walking around in the mud.

It was good someone, me, had the sense to let the girls practice. It's impressively tough to maneuver through all this squish while trying to both look good and sell stuff. The slipping, sliding, and spattering happened a lot more than anyone expected, and as a result so did the hosing downs. I saw this after two hours on the first day on the farm, and at that last minute, I doubled up the hosing stations and got the girls into flats with gripper soles. That caused some screams, but I stuck to my guns, and by the end of the second day of practicing, it was the common sense.

< < < * > > >

The concert itself went smoothly. Day Two was something of a slack day for both Ruby and me, so we managed to catch a lunch together.

Day Three I flaunted. Instead of hanging around near "the pit", I waved my Entertainer's Special Pass that Ruby had given me and experienced the whole rain shower affair from a clean, comfortable, relaxing box seat with a wonderful view of both the performance and the Statue of Liberty. Ruby, of course, was backstage at this time. This was her day.

Ruby was impressive. Her specialty was combining her good dancing and singing skill with some really impressive, supporting creation stunts. The buzz was she did a lot of the creation programming herself, and she did it with a wonderful sense of humor. It was inspired by those old, goofy comedy acts you could catch on the nostalgia channels. I watched her and laughed my ass off.

And then it was over. The creations would take care of the clean-up. We humans would attend the raucous post-production party while we waited for the first post-show reviews to come in. This time they were good for both Ruby and me. She got mentioned; my girls showed up well—gliding effortlessly and prominently through that muddy chaos on the news and entertainment vids of concert highlights.

The next day would bring some relaxing. Then planning would start, or continue, for the next performances.

Ruby's Mars Tour

"You mean send your body to Mars, not take an avatar there?"

Ruby nods vigorously. "Yeah! This is the real thing."

"Wow! That's terrific! How did you arrange that?"

"The people on Mars like their entertainment, and they're willing to pay well for it.

"They like live entertainment, and they can tell. Part of it is the gravity. You move so differently. You can simulate that, and you can "cheat" by going to the moon and performing on a stage there. It's low G, too, and a lot quicker and cheaper to get to. But those Mars people can tell, and they like paying for the real thing. They also like the after-the-performance parties, and given the many minutes turnaround for even the fastest communication links, that's real hard for an avatar to engage in," she grins.

"When will you go?"

Ruby frowns, "That's a big issue. The Mars trip will cut a giant hole in my schedule. It still takes most of a year to get there, and the same to get back. It really has to be worth my while. These are my prime years as an entertainer."

"How about in one of those new plasma jet ships? I hear they are much faster."

Ruby brightens, "Really? Are they ready?"

"I was just talking with Adrian about them a couple of days ago. Let's check..." We both consult with our searchers and confirm that plasma jet ships were going to be available to handle commercial flights next year.

"But look at the cost!" gasps Ruby. "If I'm doing this, my promoters are definitely covering that!"

Adrian's Workshop

Adrian has invited me to see his workshop. He picks me up, and to my surprise we head across the Hudson.

"Not Silicon Alley?" I comment.

"Oh, I keep a facility there," he laughs, "but I keep that one to impress investors, media people, and government committees. The one I'm taking you to now is one where I work on more interesting things.

"This is my 'mad scientist' laboratory," he says in a conspiratorial tone and grins.

My thought on that remark is, "I hope this is as funny as he seems to think it is!" I enjoy seeing science and science fiction videos every so often, and I know enough about real life to know that bioengineering is powerful stuff.

We stop somewhere in the heart of East Jersey Creationland—that industrialized area across the Hudson from Manhattan. It isn't too far from UNMSG, where Ruby had performed, but it's like being in a different world.

This place is no-nonsense. The road traffic is ninety percent or more creation traffic—so exclusively creation that no one bothers with billboards in this area. There are modest-sized company signs on some of the buildings, and some of those are logos. In this environment they look flamboyant. What is much more common is hash-code signs that creation vehicle sensors could read.

The buildings, grounds, and even the road network in all directions are spotless, mostly new, and utilitarian in design—cost/benefit, not historical legacy, determine what structures survive here.

This is quite a change from thirty years ago. Then the area had been in long-term decline and was famous for its "Jimmy Hoffa graves"—in popular media tales, the city gangsters would always dump their bodies over here somewhere. Some did in real life, too. Then twenty years ago, the creations convinced human legislators to let them handle zoning issues as well as administrative and maintenance issues in what was by then a de facto cluster of creation cities.

At first there was some protesting to that. There was legacy graft, unspoken about, and legacy buildings which became the graft's proxy and were talked about a lot. But as the creations put it, "You want to experience legacy? Get virtual in a historic sim, and get some serious and authentic legacy." How the graft got handled I'm not sure, but I do know that there were only a thousand or so voting residents left at that time, and even the nomads had abandoned the area. So even the graft pickings were pretty thin. So why not let the creations have this lemon?

Constant change has been going on in the area since the creations got full control. This ongoing cost/benefit reorganization of the local infrastructure has considerably reduced the general human impact on the environment—efficiency does that. Reduced impact, plus a whole lot of stuff now gets made here again. It's a resurgent manufacturing center. The creations have made some sweet, sweet, lemonade here.

Nowadays it's actually a bit difficult for a human to get into this area. You need a creation-issued permit. This keeps out the "Stick it to The Man" nomads, other pranksters, and outright looters. Adrian must be a regular here because we travel through various checkpoints without interruption. We stop in the parking lot of a building labeled Andy-573's Workshops and head for a door. The building looks like an oversized cheap motel—just walls and doors around a parking area, and those doors alternate between big and small. We go in one of the small doors, and I find myself in a spartan office.

"Give me five minutes," Adrian says as he dashes for his desk after opening the door.

I know the feeling, so I'm patient. I look around while he does his catch-up. He stays busy at it, and if he's anything like me, it will be more like fifteen minutes. So I do some catch-up myself, then I start wandering around the office and getting acquainted with his little wonderland here. He doesn't seem to mind.

It is clearly a human office, not a creation office. It's messy, there's stuff scattered, and half-completed projects and ideas fill a couple of tables and many shelves. And it is utilitarian. There's no brag wall here, no Feng Shui stuff, no art. I get the feeling I'm looking at some DIYer's workshop basement on steroids.

It turns out I'm not far off on that guess. When Adrian gets back to me, he shows me around and explains what we're looking at. It truly is a collection of inventor dreams.

"There is still so much to discover," Adrian says, "and like Thomas Edison said, 'Invention is one percent inspiration, ninety-nine percent perspiration.' You have to try things, and try again, over and over, in different ways."

He introduces me to George-776, the creation that runs this office.

"George-776 is one of the most unhappy creations alive," he says like he is talking to a beer buddy. "He has to endure as I have him perform one wasteful experiment after another."

"It's true," says George-776, and then in a dramatic way, "but I accept it as my lot in life. I'm here to serve humanity, and we creations all serve in different ways. Many of us serve by researching and then doing things more and more efficiently… But I follow the path less taken."

Adrian laughs again, "Don't take him too seriously. He's quite aware of Gene Editors' balance sheet."

We tour and Adrian explains some of his projects. They seem pretty obscure and trivial to me—things like, can he coax a yeast culture to pay attention to the lithium ion concentration in its growth media?

When I stifle a yawn, he gets it and explains a bit more.

"The key to the experimenting I do here is to keep it fast and flexible. I don't really care about this yeast, but if I can get these controlling concepts working here, then I can apply them to much more interesting situations—things that will affect agriculture and health. After I get something working here, *then* I introduce it to the Silicon Alley office, and we build the really big show around it.

"And speaking of really big shows..." He motions for me to head into the work shop area. "This is the part George hates the worst."

We do a quick walk through, then we stop at one table with some plastic chambers filled with complex machinery and a big monitor. He flexs his arms, cracks his knuckles, and says, "Ready to be totally amazed?"

George-776 interrupts, "Excuse me, sir, but before we start, what category do I expense this under?"

Adrian looks at me with a sparkle in his eye of what I call the "man look", "The impressing-a-woman category," he says with a grin. "You'll find that under 'Macho', 'Macho Male Bullshit' to be exact."

George-776 pauses a moment before responding, "Sorry, no macho category." Then he adds helpfully, "But we creations do have a category for human bullshit, and it's rather well populated."

Adrian laughs, "Grr... I don't do this often enough... OK, put it under 'Advertising, Male Display'."

"Right," responds George-776, taking the hint, "I'll figure it out later."

What I saw really is amazing... I guess. Adrian had transformed those plastic chambers into what for all the world looks like a flea circus composed of fruit flies. There are a dozen or so observation cubes, and he loads some fruit flies from a master cage into four of them.

"First we have some fruit flies in a control situation—a normal one. Notice that when I stick in a rotten banana, they swarm over it like insects-gone-bad in some horror film."

They do. He puts a close up image on a monitor, and it really is creepy.

"Those are females laying eggs," he explains. "They live to do just that. For these females, sex is nothing compared to the thrill of egg-laying." He watchs my reaction to that, which isn't much, then continues, "But I digress, now watch this...

"In this next chamber, there is a fruit fly obstacle course: An electrified grid, like a bug zapper. These fruit flies have been raised with this zapper as part of their environment for more than a thousand generations now. They can sense it and they understand it. Watch as I turn it up." He turns up the voltage and puts a banana in. The fruit flies swarm, but don't approach the grid.

"It's at a fully lethal level, and the flies can sense this. They stay away. Now watch what happens when I turn down the voltage to a specific level that I have researched..."

I gasp, "They're dying!" As I watch, hundreds head for the grid, get hit with the zap, and either tumble to the bottom of the chamber or get stuck to the grid and fried, literally. It's a grizzly sight.

"Not all of them," Adrian says grimly. "Ninety percent will die, but ten percent will make it through and lay their eggs. These flies are well experienced with this grid, and they have evolved to adapt to it. It turns out that they survive as a species if ten percent can make it through. When they sense the voltage is low enough to permit that, they take the risk."

He turns and looks at me, still looking grim. "This is one of the harsh realities of Mother Nature's choices: She fully understands risk taking, something modern humans do not. Many people know that in Neolithic Parks lots of women die in child birth—the actual number is one in two hundred. They reflexively think that's horrible, and then without thinking any more about why this is the way it is, call for action: Stop the slaughter! They don't finish thinking about this situation and realize this is an example of Mother Nature applying risk-taking to the human condition."

Then he smiles and gets back to talking about his work, "But this is just stage setting. This isn't the interesting part. The interesting part is what this does." He holds up a bottle of some colorless liquid, and we move to the next chamber.

"I'm going to add some 'rational thinking' to the air in this chamber. And by rational I mean becoming more risk-adverse." He spritzes the air in the chamber. "This is my latest triumph. It will take about ten minutes to affect their thinking, so let me explain more about it.

"It's well known that a lot of things affect the thinking process. We learn, we have instincts, we sense our surroundings, we have hormones… They all change how we think, and the soup of which of these are active is constantly changing. This is why teaching children, and adults for that matter, is still such a by-guess and by-gosh practice. We still don't have much control over that mix. I plan to change that."

"You're going to make people more risk adverse?" I ask incredulously.

He laughs, "No! It's even bigger than that." He wiggles his eyebrows at me in his mad scientist way, "What I'm after is the tools that will let other people design all sorts of thought-altering products. I'm providing the standards—the tools—that all other thought-altering designers will use. I will be creating an entirely new industry."

I am mystified, he can tell, and he explains further, "If I was doing this in your business, the fashion business, I would be providing colors to fashion designers. There will be fashion winners and fashion losers, but both winners and losers use my colors, so I win. The new industry I would be creating is a fashion industry that used colors."

That's a lot to take in. I'm speechless, literally.

He checks his watch and looks at the chamber. "We should be ready now." He turns up the voltage and puts the banana in.

"This is the same voltage as last time, note that the fruit flies won't approach… Now I'll lower the voltage to where they have a fifty-fifty chance of making it." He does so, and the flies now take their chances. Once again there is a pile of bodies under the grid, but only half as large as last time, and a lot more flies are now happily buzzing around the banana.

"And that's it for show and tell time," says Adrian. "Any questions?"

I can sense this is big, enormous, but little more comes to mind, so I ask, "Is this, like, secret? Should I not talk about this?"

He smiles, “Talk all you want. I’ve just shown you flashy results. I haven’t shown you any of the things that are behind the curtain. And this stuff I’m showing you is at least three years away from commercialization, if not a lot more.”

< < < * > > >

We stop for ice cream on the way back. The place is on the edge of Creationland and near empty while we are there. I’m not sure who keeps the place open, who the regular customers are. Maybe there are lots of other crazy inventors like Adrian. Whoever it is, the restaurant operators aren’t concerned about adding any human touch to their presentation. We sit down, order from the menu on the table, and the food comes out on a motorized tray.

“So was your father an inventor?” I ask while we are waiting.

“He was, but I was raised to be a dancer. My folks wanted me to be someone important, someone who would make a difference.”

“I spent years at it and got pretty good, too.” He gets up and demonstrates a couple of soft-shoe routines.

“Wow! But you didn’t pursue that? You look like you could have gone far.”

He grins, “They didn’t spend all that hard-earned money on giving me dance genes and endless childhood lessons to no effect. My family was known as the Jackson Family of Alberta. It was all local stuff and very commercial. We never got a national breakout, but the pay was good. We did well, and I could still be doing that, but I was the black sheep: I used dance to pay my way into Gene Editors.

“Dance wasn’t my dream. I had an Uncle Henry who ‘polluted’ my thinking when I was in middle school. He had a workshop, and when I came visiting, we’d spend time there. He showed me that there were things, material things, that a human could create that no creation could think of. My feeling when I saw that was, ‘Such Power!’ and I realized doing that was my dream.

“When my folks figured out how much I was enjoying my time with Uncle Henry, they got concerned. We had a heart-to-heart, and they explained how much time and resource they had put into my becoming a dancer.

"'We want the best for you, and we want you to do the best for our world,' they explained. 'And famous dancer-singers have the most influence on our modern society. If you want to have the world pay attention to you, and people do the good things that you want them to do, you need to become a successful dancer and singer. It's a lot of work. We recognize that, but we've given you the best of opportunities... if you choose to take advantage of them.'

"I was a good boy, so I did what my parents asked... for many years... but I kept *my* dream." He grins, "I learned the business side of our work. I learned to deal with people and creations who have their attention on budgets, priorities, and schedules.

"And I stayed in touch with the university research scene. Julian Homeby was a colleague of one of my professors. When I got wind of the success he was having, I contacted him and offered my services as an agent/manager for marketing his IP—Intellectual Property. We got along, and he was thinking commercial enough that we did more than license, we launched a full business... Gene Editors."

"What do your parents think of all this?"

"They have mixed feelings. They are real happy that I'm happy and that I'm successful enough to get featured in industry trade publications. But those aren't anything they read regularly, so it seems like I'm off in another world to them, an irrelevant one. They still think I would have done even better if I'd stuck to the dancing."

He looks a little embarrassed when he says, "When Dad gets to drinking too much, he accuses me of torpedoing the family's chance to get the big break." He shrugs, "We all have lives to live."

We talk more, but that's pretty much the end of that session. We finish, hop in the car, and catch up some more as we head home.

Chapter Five

The Geisha

"Tonight," I tell the class, "we are going to start with a video on one of the latest surprises in baby-making technology."

I turn on the video…

Cindy's Story

My name is Mi-Sang-0110, but my friends call me Cindy. I'm sixteen years old, and I'm a sophomore at Venice Finishing Academy. I am training to become a PAA for Mr. Jules Tipton, a wealthy man who is now 93 years old.

A PAA is a Personal Android Assistant. I am made of flesh and bone and blood, but I'm not human. I was created and raised. I spent my first two months in a cow's uterus, then I was moved to an incubating vat until I was ten months old, then I was "born" and came into the care of the Venice Finishing Academy.

When we were born, there were ten in our class—Mr. Tipton was supporting all ten of us. Mr. Tipton visits us regularly. He watches us, plays with us, and teaches us—we know him, and he knows us. He knows us well enough to make choices, and those of us who did not please him for one reason or another were moved into different programs. Now there are only three in our class, but our time living at the academy is nearing completion. We will continue training, but we will move into Mr. Tipton's house and begin serving him.

We will begin to do what we were created to do—serve him, night and day—and I'm looking forward to that. I have been trained to sing and dance, cook and keep house, talk and cuddle. When I am around, Mr. Tipton will be happy, and I will help him lose his stress.

I am mostly human, but if you listen to my chest, you will hear only my breathing, no thump, thump. My flesh heart had a defect and was removed—listen to my abdomen and you will hear the soft whine of my mechanical replacement. All PAAs have an organ replacement. We can become PAAs only if we are born with a life-threatening defect and we are saved. In the eyes of the law, this makes us recycled biomaterial, and therefore not human, and subject to a different set of laws.

Few humans want to act like PAAs. Even when they do, the laws make it difficult. A woman cannot give herself completely to a man. She can say she wants to, and she can act like she wants to, but if she changes her mind, the law will support her change of mind, and the man she has given herself to can suffer great loss when she does. This can't happen with a PAA.

So, we are expensive, but like all human creations, we fill a need that humans can't fill as well as we can.

I have a uterus, and I have ovaries, and they are fully functional. I may have a heart defect, but my genes are some of the finest humans can design.

Mr. Tipton wants me to have babies. He's told me so. He wants me to have many babies, and he will help me make them. This is part of what I will do as a PAA. As a PAA, I will make Mr. Tipton happy any way he wants me to.

I like Mr. Tipton. He's old, but his hands are strong, and he's gentle when he touches me. He touches me and Cathy and Sarah a lot. When he comes to watch us and teach us, we end the sessions with back rubs and massages. He touches us, and we touch him. Soon, he says, he will touch me in a new way, and then my tummy will swell and I will have a baby.

I will take care of it and feed it, and it will be a human baby—a real human baby, not a PAA like me. It will be a human child of Mr. Tipton's. He and I will both be very happy.

I have to go now. Class starts again soon, and Mr. Tipton will be there!

—— End of Video ——

"What have we just seen?" I ask.

Adrian answers quickly, "A geisha… Korean I would judge by her features."

"Good, and what is a geisha?"

"She describes herself pretty well in the video. A high-tech plaything for rich old men."

"Do we have them in the US?"

"Not many… yet."

"Anyone else like to contribute?"

"They aren't human. They look human, but they aren't human." It's Annette. She's come with Don this time. He's kind of bug-eyed. It could be the video or just all the new sights and sounds of the big city. She doesn't look happy about what she has seen. "I'd heard of them, but this is my first time seeing one." She pauses before saying this next part, "According to my community leaders, they are an abomination."

Ben jumps in, "The jury is still out on that here in the US, isn't it. They are in the news, now, and there are a lot of people unhappy with the PAA concept. The People Firsters are carrying the torch, but there's a lot of average women who seem to be backing them up."

"Where are they legal?" I ask.

Now Jaden jumps in, "The concept started in Japan. That's why they got the geisha moniker. It's not surprising. Japan is one of the 'grayest' places in the world. Those old Japanese men wanted better play toys, but their culture frowns on immigrants."

"Can we have them in the US?"

Jaden frowns, "There are no laws yet, one way or the other. So, you can have them… now… but there's no telling what their status will be here in the future. They could be declared human, they could be declared things, they could be granted their own status somewhere in between… that's what's happening to them in Japan.

"If they turn out to be things, then killing one is simply destruction of property. Here in the US, this problem looks a lot like the slavery problem did before the Civil War."

Janet muses, "You're right, Dahlia. It sure is an interesting surprise use."

Ben has a thought and laughs, then says like a cranky old grandpa, "In my day we had to chase a woman a mile… up hill… both ways… in the rain."

We all laugh at that, and I bring up the topic of the day and we continue on with the class.

Miranda's Interesting Offer

Miranda An lives in Astoria. It is close to Manhattan, but it's a place that has seen better times—much better times, at least in terms of its attractiveness as a place for humans to live. It is now something of a human outpost wedged between two sections of Queens devoted to industry and shipping, which means those areas are mostly creation-populated.

The people who live there are poor, but need access to the city center for one reason or another. It is a mix of students attending the city center schools, immigrants in the process of fitting in, and nomads—street people who move regularly from city to city, often calling themselves homeless.

These homeless aren't really homeless, not these days, but calling themselves homeless is good marketing because it gets them more handouts. Officially, they are now called nomads because they have city-provided shelter over their heads, but they move often from city to city. These people spend their working hours begging. Street begging is one of those traditional human occupations that technology has changed very little. They fan out to various high-traffic locations and do various low-skill activities to attract handouts. What is different these days is the numbers: The nomads are a substantial portion of the population compared to what they were even fifty years ago.

I guess it's a little unfair to call everything they do low-skill. Some are accomplished street entertainers, but a whole lot are MSH's—Masters of Sign Holding. They aren't fools, either—they are unionized and engaged in incessant turf wars among themselves for prime begging locations. This makes them somewhat violence prone. That is well-recognized, but it seems to be a necessary evil to tolerate them and their rights.

The local stay-at-home street people do some begging, too, and many odd jobs that require warm bodies, not creations. The difference between them and the nomads is the nomads wander more. They migrate regularly from city to city. Many are more delusional in one way or another. The optimistic ones feel they are here on a mission. What the mission is isn't clear and is different for each of them, but it keeps their spirits up and makes them different from "the losers"—at least in their own minds.

The pessimistic ones engage in the traditional human ways of escaping from harsh reality, such as overindulging in alcohol and various drugs, orgy partying, and getting fanatic for emotion-based causes. Here there is a sort of arms race. Medicine can combat many of the ravages of drink and drug excess, but when it does, the reality escaping doesn't work very well, either.

In their pessimistic times, these people alternate between stupor and manic raging, between wandering the streets and rehab. This part of town has seen a boom in government-supported rehab centers and ER-based hospitals, and these provide a lot of employment for semi-reformed and older nomads. They become first-level social workers and therapists.

The students here tend to dodge the nomads. Most feel the nomads are serious losers and to be avoided like the plague, some feel they are serious losers and deserve some sympathy, and a few feel they are serious losers and targets for bullying. Did I mention this neighborhood is violent?

And then there are the immigrants, like Miranda, who are here trying to figure out how our United States works, and finding their place to fit into it.

All-in-all... Whew! What a mix!

I meet Miranda at a neighborhood coffee house, not her home. This is partly because of tradition in her home country, partly because she is living with her family and some fellow immigrants in a cramped apartment, and partly because she says there are some pretty aggressive beggar-types that haunt the street in front of her place. She comes with her mother and a friend and we have a round of introductions as coffee is ordered up and served. Before the coffee is served, the friend gets a call and apologizes that she has to rush off. I think she'd come mostly just so they were a crowd as they walked down the street, and they get less flack that way.

The coffee Miranda drinks has an odd aroma. I presume it is some brew local to her homeland. We've been in class together enough now that I know she is a good girl, and ambitious, so I figure this is a popular regional drink, not some new designer stimulant—which it could easily be in a place like this.

"I wanted to talk with you outside of class... and with my mother... because I've received a job offer."

"That's wonderful news!" I say.

"It's from Mr. and Mrs. Hosker," she continues. "They want me to be a surrogate mother for them."

"... They want you to bear the child, as well as raise it?"

Miranda nods.

"Mrs. Hosker is worried that her womb may be too old," she says. "She has stopped having regular periods, you know. Plus, they are planning to have the fertilization done in a test tube, anyway. They want to be real sure they are getting a good... zygote." This is still a new word for her, so she stumbles over it a bit. "Since all this is happening outside her womb, they figure they may as well pick a good womb to put this new baby back into... And that's what they want me to do."

I'm a little bit surprised, but just a little. The Hoskers seem like no-nonsense types, and this is a no-nonsense plan.

While I consider what she has told me, she explains to her mother what she has just explained to me. The mother's face is wrinkled and care-worn, and it shows even more concern as she listens. Clearly where she comes from, she has been poor and the culture is still poor. She hasn't learned English and she hasn't had access to any skin protection.

"How do you feel about it?" I ask when she turns back to me.

"Well... I was planning to be a baby raiser. But I was also planning on getting married and raising my own children." She looks at her mother who nods vigorously.

"Mother and I are not sure how this would affect that."

"If I may ask, are you still a virgin?"

"Oh yes," she says reflexively, and I believe it. It is still important in her culture.

"So... part of the questions is, if I am correct, will you still be a virgin if you get a zygote implant?"

She nods and looks down. "I will not have known a man, but..."

Her mother speaks up quietly using her broken English, "This is dinky dau!"

"She means this is crazy," Miranda explains. Worry is all over the mother's face now.

"Have you asked your religious person?" I ask.

"Oh, I am a Christian... Buddhist-Christian, actually. I talked to my new reverend here in the city. He is a good man. He thought about it and said, 'You know, I don't know.'"

As we are talking, a commotion starts outside and grows louder. I walk to the window and look out. There are people marching down the street carrying signs. It's a protest of some sort. Riot control creations are already lining up on the street sides with their big shields.

"Best to stay inside for now," advises the shopkeeper, who comes up beside me. "These are usually just noisy... usually."

Even as she speaks, there is a flash of ugly violence. Right in front of the store a young man is thrown down and held there until police and restraint creations gather around and arrest him. The shopkeeper goes to the door and yells out to find out what has happened. She is careful to stay inside—the protest is still very much in progress.

She listens, then turns to us and reports, "That boy was a gypsy. Apparently he and his buddies were lifting wallets. This protest was providing great distraction... they thought! Ha!" she ends triumphantly.

"The gypsies are not well-liked around here," Miranda confides, standing on my other side. "They come and go, and they are competition to the regulars."

As they lift the boy up to carry him away, I get a good look at him. He is so innocent-looking—probably fourteen, wavy hair, dewy eyes, clear skin.

“He’s just a child!” I exclaim without thinking.

“Not likely!” huffs the shopkeeper. She looks at me and says knowingly, “He’s Roma. They learned long ago that strangers will let kids get away with anything. These days they use every medical trick they can afford to prolog that kid look. He’s probably twenty-one and been grifting for a decade now.”

I look back at her in disbelief.

“I’m not kidding.” She looks up and down the street, then points at an odd-looking man standing in a shadow not far away. He is a medium-set dwarf, and his face has the mask-look of many overdone facelifts. “That’s likely the boy’s handler. He’s what you look like when the medicine can’t keep up.”

I try getting an ID on this strange-looking man. The answer comes back: “Mr. John Jones, Groton, Connecticut.” That sure doesn’t seem right. I show it to the shopkeeper.

More huffing. “They routinely steal IDs. First, they claim they are being persecuted, so they get a special anonymous and changeable ID. Then they take it to one of the local hacker shops and start adding real IDs they have stolen.”

She looks at me once more to summarize, “These are not nice people. Keep your distance from them, Honey.”

About that time, the media truck rolls up. There is a perfunctory interview where the leader of the protest explains what this one is about. When the interview is finished, a few of the protesters in a photogenic area throw vegetables at the riot control creations. The creations respond by advancing menacingly for about ten feet, banging batons on their shields, and the vegetable-tossers scatter. And that’s it. It all breaks up. It takes about twenty minutes, total.

In the aftermath, protesters fill the coffee house. The shopkeeper heads off to service the rush, and Miranda and I sit down with her mom again.

“Do you mind if I call the Hoskers about this?” I ask Miranda.

“Not at all,” she says.

I make contact with Ben. He is at home. When I explain what’s up, he calls Janet and they both get online. They are both sitting together on a sofa in their home.

“We would have contacted you about this next, Dahlia, if there was any more to talk about. And it sounds like there is. Excellent." Ben has an easy, self-assured manner about him, and Janet looks fully supportive. She speaks up next.

"To fill you in a little more, two things have come up since the class began. First, I've been consulting with my doctors, and I guess I'm a little more 'over the hill' than I thought I was. The womb therapy to get me fertile again would take many months, and I would likely have several spontaneous abortions before I have a success. Sadly, even with what we know today, for me carrying a child to full term is still a dicey proposition.

"Secondly, we've received an offer to do some charity work. It's an interesting offer, but it involves traveling to Africa, and that would interfere with my womb therapy."

Ben concludes for both of them, "So… we still want to raise a child, want to very much, but it looks like we may have to do it by alternative methods. And that's why we contacted Miranda with our proposal."

While Ben and Janet have been talking, both the noise level and the aroma level in the coffee house has been rising. The protest is over, but the celebrating of "sticking it to the man" will go on quite a bit longer. It is getting distracting, and there are a couple of celebrants eyeing our half-empty table.

"Why don't you come over here?" suggests Ben.

It sounds like a good idea, so we break off our conversation and head out. On the way out and all the way to the taxi, we get pestered:

"Support the cause," with a hand out.

"Sign my petition and donate," with a sheet of paper and a hand out.

The worst is when a scruffy-looking man with a good-looking face gets up from his chair suddenly and blocks my way. "Stick it to the man!" he says. Then instead of just holding his hand out in front of me, he reaches his hand up beside my ear, "… I take credit cards." When his hand comes back in front of me, it has a credit card in it! It's the old magic coin trick updated.

He holds the card in front of me for a good two seconds.

The shopkeeper yells at him, "Carlos! Give it a break! This isn't Times Square." He grins, laughs harshly, and sits back down to continue celebrating with his friends. Sheesh! I bet he's been waiting all week to try that stunt! But it is more sinister than that, too. If I'd grabbed for that card, he could have accused me of credit card theft, and it would have happened in front of a dozen witnesses. This cheap trick is a new Times Square scam. The accusation would go through a creation-run legal mill, get settled out of court, and I'd be getting paycheck deductions to support that creep!

We don't look amused as we walked by. Clearly this isn't our territory, and these people are nothing like the helpful strangers Andy and I had met in Butterfield Canyon.

The taxi ride to the Hoskers is uneventful, as usual. Creation drivers don't get bored or speak in thick foreign accents, unless they sense you're a foreigner or need some advice. Enroute I do have to add some instructions to my message bot. Apparently I'd been ID'd in the coffee house, and I am now getting "donate to my cause" spam from those protesters in the coffee house. My goodness, they could be a pain!

The Hoskers place is plush. It is high up with a good view and furnished with a mix of high-design Scandinavian and hand-crafted African. We sit in the living room and get more acquainted. Ben starts.

"I retired last year as the NYC-region VP of Stock-SMart, number six retailer in the world. There was a management shakeup, and I was on the losing side." He shrugs, "The new guys are hot-shot outsiders who think we were wasting resources and still in the Stone Age in our decision-making style. They plan on bringing in creations to handle higher levels of management.

"I wish them luck, but the merchandise selecting in retail is still a people business. I think they are in for a rude awakening.

"I could have moved to a similar position with another organization. I had offers... serious offers. But it's time for a change. It's time to do a legacy project. A lot of people in my position who make this choice say they are leaving to spend time with their family. I guess I'm leaving to make my family to spend time with!" He smiles at Janet, rubs her leg a bit. She takes her turn.

"I'm a career negotiator. I graduated from Wellesley, got work in the State Department for fifteen years, and then moved on to various projects for NGOs. The highlight of my State Department work was being chief negotiator for the China-US trade agreement of 2098.

"Now, as Ben mentioned to you, we are about to get involved in another Africa project: Improving the conditions of the rural people living in South Sudan. These are some of the poorest people left on earth—outside of the Neolithic Villages, of course. The project will involve a lot of travel and some rough living conditions. That's why we've been in contact with Miranda." She smiles at Miranda in a nice way.

"We want our child. And we want it to be the best we can produce. We think Miranda helping out—right from the start, if you will—will improve our child's opportunities and give Miranda some deeper bonding with it as she raises it. We see it as win-win."

Ben takes over again smoothly. I can see why they have a reputation for being quite the team.

"We recognize that this is an unusual extension of the usual child-raising practice. And we recognize that it may conflict with Miranda's," then looking at her mother, "or her family's cultural or personal ethics. So we will not be upset if she declines. We will still offer her the opportunity to raise the child. But, if she wants to get more involved, we will be deeply appreciative, in many ways."

I am impressed. It is an interesting offer and presented in a competent and sincere way. I know *I* am getting warm fuzzies over what I'm hearing. I look at Miranda and her mother. They are both looking unsettled and talking quietly to each other in their native tongue. The Hoskers are patient.

Miranda finally answers, "We… I thank you very much for this offer, Ben and Janet." She is still a bit uncomfortable with using their familiar names. "My mother and I will discuss this further."

The Hoskers look satisfied with this answer. "Are there any more questions we can answer for you at this time?" asks Ben.

Miranda checks with a look at her mom, "I think we have plenty to think about for right now." she says.

There are a few more pleasantries then the meeting breaks up and we all head elsewhere.

Chapter Six

Visiting a Neolithic Park

It's another one of those crazy fashion promoting ideas, but not that crazy: Doing a promotion with a Neolithic Park background.

It's crazy because Neolithic Parks are all about low-tech and self-sustaining. Their high fashion is grinding up charcoal and ochre rocks, mixing the powders with animal fat, and spreading them over various parts of the body. Well… that and tattoos… without decent needles and anesthetics! Brrr! I shudder just thinking about that!

It's not that crazy because people are always gaga about what happens in Neolithic Parks. It's so famously one-with-nature—yet so alien!

The real Neolithic Parks are strictly off-limits to civilized folk. The feeling is that any contact with civilized folk will pollute their self-sustainability, and that's the whole reason to have them.

But the strong curiosity is still there. As a result, there is a thriving industry of Neolithic Park simulations. The simulations come in dozens of formats: There are simple and safe Neolithic Park simulations at most amusement parks—many are simply petting zoos. There are sim and avatar worlds which look a lot more dangerous. Many adventure/thriller stories feature a romp through one. And there are full-fledged Neolithic Park camps where a person can pit their human selves one-on-one against nature… with a lot of supervision and a clinic nearby.

The challenge for us at DeMuzzy is how to look fresh with this concept. It's popular, but so overdone! I'm handed the task of surveying our park background options.

I first research as close to the root as I can: I contact the Ministry of Neolithic Parks and get an online briefing from Grace-224 on the situation in the real parks. These are an eye opener. Grace-224 shows me videos from previous studies and some views with real-time surveillance cameras. It is pretty clear that genuine is not going to be any good as a DeMuzzy display format. These people live in camps and the camps are… grubby is probably the best way to describe them. Just terrible as a fashion background! Plus, we can't be there in person, so if there is anything inspiring there, we'd have to simulate.

Grace-224 explains, "The security around the parks is quite high and surprisingly busy. All sorts of people try to penetrate the parks and try routinely."

"Really? Why?"

"There are a variety of motives. Some are there on a dare. Some are there to help these people out of their misery—they completely ignore the charter. Some come and bring trinkets—they seem to love being gods to these people. Some come to shoot vids and trade for authentic crafts work which they then sell on the outside, even though that is illegal."

"The penalties for getting caught in one are minor, so our vigilance must be high."

Interesting to me, but not too important to the project. What is important to the project is the look of the people. Gag! They are gaunt, diseased, scarred, and crippled: I want to scream and hide when I see one smile—those mouths! The only fashion for this place is horror fashion! What virtue does anyone see in this?

The virtue, as the briefing pointed out, is that these people survive with their own technology. If the civilized world collapses for any reason, these people are our best hope for survival because they truly don't need anything civilized, nothing at all. "They are an insurance policy," the creation notes, "and as such they will seem expensive until the disaster they are designed to protect against happens."

OK, no help for us there. I next research a couple of Neolithic experience camps. These are the places that let civilians get as close to the Neolithic experience as they want to. These, too, are rather unsettling. Many of them seem to be run by sadists. Their promotions talk a lot about "building character" and "finding your measure against nature". These pitches seem very popular with some teenagers and their parents. Others -- amazing to me—are actually popular as a course in management training. They pitch "bonding" and "leadership experience". I watch people go through a lot of what seem like hazing rituals conducted in the woods and listen to the happy participants endorse the experience, and again, it is unsettling. Personally, I can relate to those people who come out unhappy and complain of brainwashing.

This camp stuff looks nothing like what the real park people are experiencing—the whole point seems quite different. These "experience" people have a lot more in common with the martial arts crowd and the military basic training crowd than the park people. The park people only put up with what they can't avoid. They don't go looking for misery. In sum, I just don't think we can get the right feel if we stage at one of these. Next...

The Neolithic avatars and sims are all about making an entertainment experience of the setting. They are about being beautiful in a beautiful nature setting. And, once again, they seem to be missing the point in favor of catering to a popular demand. But at least these settings are about beauty and romantic wonder. In my heart I like them, and in my non-work life, I spend time off in a couple.

So... with all these Neolithic-themed experiences selling out, should DeMuzzy be any different? Given the above choices, it would be quick and easy to strut our stuff in some avatar setting, and that entertainment-oriented setting would be quite compatible with fashion. It is so easy that avatar runway settings are common, a sub-industry in fact. The biggest problem with not being any different would be... we wouldn't be any different! But we're DeMuzzy! We're about being leaders, not "me too"!

As usual, it's a big challenge, and I don't have a quick answer.

The weekend is fast approaching, so I leave this as something to solve next week. What is coming this weekend is a visit to Grandma Heather.

The Avatar Cruise Ship

Time for a visit with Grandma Heather. And as is common, she was on the *Festivia 8* when visit time comes. I join her there.

The *Festivia 8* is an avatar cruise ship. It travels endlessly around the Gulf of Mexico and Caribbean, stopping at exotic ports of call. Well, at least that's what it advertises. Personally, I find the ship and the ports of call as exotic as traveling around Disney World, which should not be too surprising since Disney runs the line. But that's me, not Grandma Heather. She and her current husband, Frank, eat this experience up with a spoon.

The *Festivia 8* is behemoth class: It was the biggest passenger ship in the world when it was launched ten years ago. Well, it would have been if it had passengers. The *Festivia 8* has no people on it—none. It's completely creation run and avatar inhabited. That keeps the cost way down. That's partly why Heather and Frank like it. They spend lots of time there, so cost is a consideration. And for reasons that escape me entirely, they like the bigness. There are many other choices: There are smaller ships and ships with mixed populations and some that are small and mostly human that go to truly exotic places, such as around the Bay of Bengal and the Antarctic coast. But Heather and Frank are *Festivia* fans, and proud of it.

I join them by inhabiting a guest avatar, and find them beside the pool. The day is bright and sunny, and the air is warm and filled with sea scent. My guest avatar is non-descript female—not quite as plain as a "generic with just an ID number on the forehead to distinguish" avatar, but not much more. The regulars, such as Heather and Frank, spend much of their time on board customizing their avatars—think of it as sending your own body to a beauty spa—and avatar customizing is definitely part of the cruise experience. In their case the results are pretty impressive, and in fact, they have been featured in a couple of movies that were shot on the *Festivia*.

Movie shooting is just one of hundreds of activities that people do on board—you meet people here who share interests, and I guess that's the secret to the cruise ship industry's popularity.

The three of us spend some time catching up while we're poolside. Frank likes to talk politics, and he starts right in.

"So... did you see the results of the elections in South Sudan?" he asks me.

"No," I reply, "something interesting?"

"They kicked out the current government. The winners claim it was corrupt and a stooge for multinational corporations."

"Sounds good."

"Sounds good, but I hear the people making those claims know well what they are talking about... because they are crooked as a dog's hind leg."

"That doesn't sound good! Funny you should mention that because I know some people who will be going to South Sudan for some charity work. Should they be concerned?"

"I would!" he says. "But then again, I wouldn't go to South Sudan even in an avatar. Someone would probably kidnap it, and I'd have to pay to replace it. That's a pretty rough part of the world these days."

"I'll bring that up with my acquaintances," I say. And I will. I sure don't want something bad happening to Janet or Ben. I'm sure they know what they are getting into, but I'll double check.

To change the topic, I inquire politely how Grandma's physical body is doing. I'm careful because this can be a touchy subject among avatar people—some don't want to talk about their physical at all. But I'm family and Grandma is not one of the touchy kind.

"Oh, it's doing fine," she says. "I had an operation last week to work on some hearing issues, and my arthritis is staying calm. It's doing fine."

I'm happy to hear that, and happy to hear she's still spending serious energy on keeping it up. Some avatar lovers are pretty neglectful. They let their healthcare creations handle all the body-running details while they put all their attention into running their avatars.

We finish the catch-up with a bit of swimming. Frank shows off a new dive he has mastered—not bad for a ninety-three year old, even if it is an avatar body. Then we go inside for some lunch. It's semi-formal. We dress, which takes about half a second, and sit around a table with other avatar folk on the cruise and do some more getting acquainted. The food is just avatar sim, of course, but it's tasty, and the ritual of dining is comfortable, and the conversation and people meeting are stimulating.

As the social etiquette people constantly point out, meeting avatars is a different skill than meeting people face-to-face and a different skill from one meeting place to the next. In a place like *Festivia,* designing what your avatar looks like is half the fun, so it's perfectly OK to comment on another person's latest design triumph. If this was a business boardroom avatar meeting, or an engineering conference meeting, or an at-a-jobsite meeting, you wouldn't say a thing about looks. But here it's just fine.

Here at the *Festivia* dining tables, there is an enormous mix in what people do in real life. About three quarters are retired, and for about half of those, *Festivia* ***is*** real life—they spend most of their time and most of their attention here and are totally wrapped up in on-ship activities. For the other half, this is a diversion from what they do in real life with their physicals, or in some other work-oriented avatar environment where they are still earning pay or good karma as a volunteer. The last quarter are younger. Some are real-life cripples, and like the dedicated oldsters, this is their life. Others are just hanging out for a long weekend or short vacation. There is also a steady stream of short-stay family and friend visitors, such as myself, who inhabit the guest avatars.

One of the guests at our table is Lucas Hansen, mayor of Provo-Orem. My geography is outstanding for a city girl. I know that's a city in Utah, and Utah is in the Rocky Mountains… somewhere.

"Provo-Orem?" I comment. "I haven't heard much about it. How is it holding up these days?"

"Quite well, thank you. The city is growing in population and we've been thriving. The ski industry is good and we've been getting lots of adventure entertainment shot in the area."

"That sounds more avatar-oriented, if I may say so. You say it's growing… What brings the people?"

He grins at that. "Where are you from, if I may ask?"

"New York City," I reply. "I work there with DeMuzzy High Fashion. Let me introduce myself. I'm Dahlia Rose." As I am talking, I make my business resume available to him online.

He pauses a moment to absorb the resume highlights then says, "A pleasure to meet you, Dahlia. To answer your question: What keeps Provo-Orem growing is its natural beauty and the Mormon culture that thrives there. The lifestyle there is different from Big Apple lifestyle."

"Oh... like polygamists and such?" my grandmother interjects.

He laughs at that, "We do have them these days. Polygamy had been outlawed in the state for two hundred years, but twenty years ago the practice became legal again.

"But no, that's not the heart of it. The heart is the clean living and faith-oriented lifestyle that is popular in the area. Some people accuse us of running America's largest cult city. It may feel like that if you're from a more cosmopolitan area, such as New York, but I assure you, it's still a quite open and quite American way of living. We like to think of ourselves as the 'Other Aspen'—we are more wholesome family oriented, rather than personal fulfillment oriented." He smiles in conclusion.

Then it hits me, "Is that close to Butterfield Canyon?"

"The one in the Oquirrh Mountains, overlooking Bingham Canyon Copper Mine and Salt Lake City? Yes, about a thirty minute drive south. You may have spotted Mount Timpanogos, our valley's signature peak, from the overlook, if you've been there."

"Ah... yes. I visited there with my ex-boyfriend—had quite an adventure there, too. You're right. It's truly a spectacular area for scenery. I'm happy to hear humans are thriving in the area, as well.

"... In fact," I continue because I've just had an "Ah hah", "You and your wonderful scenery may be able to help me out on a project. Would you mind if I contacted you further on a business arrangement?"

"I'd be delighted," he says, and we exchange business contact information.

My thought is that colorful scenery in Utah might be a suitable substitute for a Neolithic Park setting for our fashion show. We'd go Wild West in place of Neolithic Park. It can have that same individualistic and one-with-nature theme. The big plus is that Utah scenery is quite photogenic—and different!

Grandma carries on the conversation, "We've had some of your Mormons speak at our seminars in Chautauqua, New York. They had some interesting ideas about Christianity. I don't recall them talking at all about polygamy."

"The mainstream church still doesn't believe in it," replied Lucas, "but there are over twenty fairly large groups that have splintered off from the main church over the years, and a few of those do. Those groups used to be centered in many different places around the US, Canada, and Mexico, and some of them still are—those that are survivalist as well as fundamentalist. Many of the rest have steadily migrated back into the Utah area. They find the culture more comfortable than the cosmopolitan areas. So there are a few in the area, but you have to look hard to spot them."

The conversation then drifts on to other things. I have a good time, and it is good to spend some time with Grandma.

Ruby's Proposition

I enjoyed working with Rubyzin on her book project, and it seems she did too. She invited me to help her with another project, and I got her a couple of guest appearances at our presentations.

Then comes the kicker. She invites me to dinner one night after the Paris Fashion Show had run its course, and we at DeMuzzy are on a recovery time. "Girl's night out," she announces in her text. The week in Paris had been the usual frantic, but it had gone well, and now this was just the kind of relaxing that I need.

We meet at Da Munchie's. In spite of the hokey name, it is a place with a solid reputation among the old wealth. It's quiet and paparazzi are not welcome.

"This is a place where I can let my hair down a bit," confides Ruby.

After we order, Ruby gets to the point.

"Dahlia, there's another project I want to propose we join forces on: our baby making."

I am a little surprised, but just a little. I know Ruby does things for good reasons; she is not the success she is because she wastes time or energy.

"You're not a teacher at Child Champs for no reason. And over the last few weeks, I've found you good to work with. So... let's work on the big one together," she concludes with a smile and a touch of my hand.

"It's an interesting possibility, Ruby. What exactly do you have in mind? Who else would be involved?"

"I'm proposing we set up shop together. I don't have a boyfriend at this point. Of course I've met a lot of studly, virile types… some of those dancers… Whew! The muscles and the moves!… But I haven't found one I'd feel comfortable waking up with day-after-day. They're good and they know it. But they come across as so self-centered, and yet no business sense! In my heart, I'm a business lady.

"Which is why I'm talking to you. I sense simpatico with you, Dahlia." She touches me again, and I admit, it doesn't feel bad at all. This is a powerful woman whom I respect. And over the last few weeks and projects, I'd come to respect her even more. This proposal is certainly flattering, if nothing else!

I touch her back as I say, "Wow!… In truth I don't know what to say, Ruby. I'm certainly honored, and I've enjoyed your company very much…. This is just way outside of how I was figuring I'd get into baby making."

Ruby smiles. "I'm not surprised. And I didn't expect a 'Yes! Yes!' and big kiss," she laughs, "but I wanted to start you thinking along these lines.

"If we team up, we can do this in a business-like way, and we can get our kids the best of everything… *everything*." Her eyebrows arch as she says that. "I've been researching who makes the best DNA and who makes the best wombs. I think you've researched who offers the best child-raising services. To my mind, this is going to be my real legacy, not my performances or my businesses, so I want it to be my best."

"You're not planning on carrying your own child?"

She frowns a bit. "I've given this a lot of thought. I want to. And in truth, I worry that my baby won't know me if it hasn't spent time inside me. But I've been assured that that's not the case. And, as I said earlier, I'm a businesswoman at heart. Business is important, and I haven't figured out how to keep my career moving with a baby swelling up inside me." She looks into my eyes, this time with some sorrow showing, and touches me again, looking for support. "This isn't the fun part."

Then she brightens a bit. "That's why I want to team with you."

"Do you mind if I carry mine?" I ask.

"Not at all! I'd be delighted! It's something we can share." She brightens more, "And we can get you the best-of-the-best, too. We can have kids that will rock this world!" She smiles warmly at that thought, gets up and actually comes over to give me a little hug, and then sits down again.

It sure is good that this isn't a paparazzi place. We finish our dinner, both feeling warm and fuzzy. I'm not sure I want to pick up on this project in the real world, but I'm sure enjoying thinking about it as a possibility as we talk this evening.

My mind is singing, "Me and Ruby and baby makes three… no, four!" LOL! We sure could rock this world!

Chapter Seven

Jaden Plays Santa

"So, do you have any holiday plans, Jaden?" asks Jaina.

"Yeah! I just scored a neat gig. I'm going to be a Santa Claus at a mall in Queens. I'll be there a couple days a week during Christmas vacation, and the pay is good! It's going to finance a nice vacation to Paris next summer. I'll go the Art Institute there and take a course on Post-Impressionism."

"Mmm... sounds like a nice double benefit!"

"Yeah. I don't mind being around young kids, and getting to research the French masters by seeing their work in person is a real turn-on for me! And Paris... mmmm."

"So did the school arrange this?" I ask.

"No. It was a job one of my fellow teachers had arranged earlier this year, but he got transferred to Washington over the summer. He'd totally forgotten about this until he got a confirmation call. He posted on the school site, and I picked it up."

"Neat!" says Jaina.

Gray Areas

"This lesson is a continuation of the topic we started in the geisha lesson: the gray areas of baby making. Gene scientists have made a lot of advancements in the last decade. Ninety-nine percent of these have nothing to do with baby raising, but that last one percent gets a lot of news and a lot of discussion.

"One code that has been mastered recently is enzyme sequence that brings on puberty."

"The key to stopping aging?" asks Jaden hopefully.

"Many people would like it to be so, Jaden, but no. It just stops puberty. The early test animals it's been employed on seem to stay young, and in fact, they keep growing… and growing. In the early demonstrations they grew goldfish to the size of tuna. As the growth gets into that huge size range, the fish's circulation system finally just kind of disintegrates—it was never designed for such volume. So the breakthrough is not anti-aging but it should produce profitable applications in agribusiness."

"Cheap goldfish sandwich at last!" wisecracks Ben. I continue.

"But that hasn't stopped many people from wishing and hoping, and gray area types from preying on those wishes and hopes. Yes, it can now be applied to humans, and Janet Van Kiester has been making news by wanting to mix the puberty stopping with growth inhibitor. She wants to make what she calls 'eternal childhood'. That's a big overstatement of what's likely to come out of her work, but it sure sounds warm and fuzzy."

"What's likely to come out?" asks Ruby.

"The body of a child that grows old. Aging is a lot more than just stopping puberty. There may be applications for this ability. There may be environments where a child-like body suits better than adult bodies, but it's not an eternal fountain of youth. This person will still learn and become more knowledgeable as years go by, and parts of the body will still age, but, yes, there will likely be differences in thinking—no crazy-raging-hormone falling in love." I grin at that, and get some grins back from Ben and Janet. Jaina, not surprisingly, seems a bit confused.

"Sounds like it could almost produce a pet," says Ruby. Ben and Janet nod at this as well.

"Like the geisha, this is a deep concern," I agree. "Some wags are calling this the feminist answer to geishas… old men get their sex toys, old women get their child pets." Jaina giggles at this, and I continue, "This is yet another technology that will be full of surprises. What we want to do in this class is make sure we get the good surprises, or when we are going to take risks, be sure we understand as much of what is at risk as we can."

Dahlia's Visit to Annette's Home

"Dahlia, I want you to come see where I live," Annette announces to me after class.

"You've been so helpful and so tolerant of our different ways that our prophet, Isaac Jesper, would like to meet you in person."

I am honored and we set a date. The colony has no avatars so this will be an in-person visit.

The trip there is long and difficult. The nearest airport is a two-hour drive by land vehicle, and that vehicle is driven by a person. The first half is standard enough on a road we share with lots of creation traffic. The second half is something special! It is on a dirt "road"... with the driver really driving! It is a rough ride on cleared dirt—speeding up, slowing down, twisting, turning, bouncing, bouncing, BOUNCING. And the heat! Even with the air conditioner running, the heat pulses through the glass windows. The driver is wearing weathered jeans, a reed hat, and a cotton shirt, and his face skin is getting as weathered as his jeans. But he is kind, and when he notices I'm getting a bit green under the gills and losing my concentration as I try to text, he tries to steady up the ride.

"Not used to this, eh?" he says knowingly with a drawl.

"It doesn't come up often for me," I admit.

"Keep your head up. Keep looking out. And think happy thoughts. It helps," he says. "You're not the first city slicker to make this trip... and they all survived," he grins.

I put away my phone and just look out the windows. Annette had advised me that multi-tasking was frowned upon at the compound, so I might as well get used to it early. And it does help.

In fact, now that I am paying attention, I see that the driver's driving skill is impressive. He seems to be one with this vehicle and this road, and there is no creation I can see acting as intermediary.

When he pushes on the gas, the engine roars immediately; when he pushes on the brake, he is determining how much we slow down. Impressive! Prior to this my only experience with a person directly commanding a vehicle was at an amusement park ride.... Oh, and riding my bicycle at the bicycle course in the park.

I know immediately when we reach the compound. We cross over a rise, and on the far side the view is dominated by a huge white building surrounded by an immaculate green grass lawn—very out of place in the dusty, arid scrub we've been driving through.

We don't go to that building, though. We drive around it and go to a building more modest in size, but equally well maintained.

As we drive into the parking lot, the driver explains, "That's the temple. That's for the faithful. Strangers don't go in there. This here's the residence of the prophet. You'll be staying here and meeting him here."

As we get out, Annette comes out of the building and gives me a big hug. She looks so happy, relaxed and comfortable here—hardly the reserved, strong-willed matron I'm used to in class sessions. The driver brings my bags as we walk in.

"I've scheduled you for a tour first. Then you will meet Prophet Jesper." She takes my arm as we walk in.

I get settled and toured. It is fascinating, partly because I am seeing this for the first time in person, not reviewing a VR summary. It is a strange feeling, and I have to take it slow.

Surrounding the temple and residence, these people have built homes, schools, and workshops. There are a thousand or so people living here, so it's a full community. The workshops are filled with men busy fabricating stuff. "We try to make as much as we can for ourselves," explains Annette. "We don't want creations doing what man was intended to do."

I am polite enough not to point out that all the tools these men are using were made by creations. But I am impressed with how much of the compound is taken up in workshops. It is a lot. And what they produce doesn't look like creation stuff, either. It is simpler, cruder, and has a different aesthetic. "We sell some of this to collectors and get a good price for it," Annette tells me.

We also tour a home, a school, and a social hall. As we walk from building to building, we are surrounded with children. They are all over, and going everywhere—even in this heat that is driving me batty. They seem quite used to it. There are mothers around doing some herding of the kids, but compared to what I am used to seeing, these are pretty free-ranging kids! I had also noticed a lot of pretty young-looking kids in some of those workshops. Even though back in the real world, it is strictly illegal to hire anyone under eighteen, I decide not to mention it, but Annette does.

"The workshops where you see the youngsters are not producing anything commercial," she says. "In the commercial ones, we have only eighteen year-olds and up. These kids in here are just doing hobbies."

"Part of learning human-sufficiency?" I ask. She nods. It seems like a fine line to me, but I guess they are getting away with it.

Late that afternoon, after I've had a chance to freshen up and recover a bit, I meet with the prophet.

The prophet's office is plush, but in a distinctive way. On the walls are paintings of Biblical and early American history events all done in a realist paint-on-canvas style. All the furnishings are human-crafted. They come from around the world, and many are antiques from different eras, so there is no theme other than being human crafted. To my designer eye, it looks like a collection of kitsch, like you might find in an off-the-strip Las Vegas casino lobby... different strokes for different folks.

The prophet himself, Isaac Jesper, is immaculately dressed and sits at his desk flanked by two associates. Annette quietly excuses herself after she shows me in. Annette may have to be obsequious, but it seems the prophet does not stand on formality with important strangers because once the door shuts, he gets up and meets me halfway and gives me a warm handshake.

"Ms. Rose—may I call you that—I'm so happy you accepted Annette's invitation. Please have a seat!" He motions me towards a sofa and coffee table arrangement on the side of the office halfway between the door and his desk. "Would you care for a drink?" he asks as we get seated. "You're a guest, so you're not subject to our dietary restrictions. What can I get you? Coffee, tea, soda, water, something stronger?"

I think for a moment. This colony food system isn't connected to my Diet Minder in any way. Whatever I eat here is the real deal, not customized to my current requirements, and not aware of my digestive sensitivities. Then again, my Diet Minder will compensate at my next real meal, and my gut nanotech can probably deal with whatever exotic microbes come with this territory. Then again, this is a religious issue. Whew! So innocent, but such a loaded question!

"Coffee," I decide. I don't want to look too cautious, nor do I want to look like some kind of libertine. One of the assistants heads off to prepare it.

Jesper's small talk is surprisingly pleasant. He inquires about current events happening in the Big Apple and asks about how DeMuzzy is faring, and he seems genuinely interested. I find myself warming up to him. He has charisma, that's for sure. Then he gets to the point.

"Dahlia, Annette has been quite impressed by what she is learning in her class, and with you personally. What she has brought back to the colony from your class has impressed the elders as well. We figure that if you understand a bit more about our program, it could be mutually beneficial.

"What do you know about our Reaching for Paradise colony?"

"I know that you're out here because you're not happy with the human-creation relations that characterize much of modern society." (I'd done some homework.) "I know that your group is modeled after a cul… group that broke away from the mainstream Mormon religion about two hundred years ago. I—"

"You know about the plural marriage, of course," he interrupts.

"I do. Is that still an issue?"

"The people that live out here are all religious conservatives… but in several different ways. Yes, there are people out here that take strong issue with our practice. I'm wondering… what are your feelings on that issue?"

I shrug. "Different strokes for different folks. It's not an issue that's on my radar."

He looks relieved, "That has probably helped in your relation with Annette.

"I wanted to talk with you a bit to clarify some issues with you. Those people who know about our colony, and care, tend to have both strong feelings and big misconceptions. I'd like you to get the straight skivvy."

"I'm happy to learn," I say.

"Because our belief in polygamy was shunned in the 19th and 20th centuries, our people were persecuted and forced to live in places where few other people had a desire to. As a result, we developed a lot of self-sufficiency. Seventy years ago a new crisis came up. Polygamy became acceptable in many mainstream societies, and many of the religion's members wished to relocate, and many did. These days you can find FLDS groups in Vancouver, Dallas, and San Diego."

"And Provo-Orem?" I ask.

Isaac smiles. "The mainstream Mormons are still a bit too close to this issue to be comfortable with us. The FLDS there keep a low profile."

"You're saying you're not FLDS?"

"No, we are not. The church split in the crisis I was just talking about. We declared them apostates and they declared us excommunicated. It got ugly. There were property issues as well as doctrinal ones. If they were leaving places like Hildale and the YFZ ranch behind, we wanted them. In the end, with God's blessing, we compromised. I won't go into the details."

"So... what was the issue?" I was getting confused.

"Those of us remaining here received the revelation that polygamy wasn't the big issue—it was self-sufficiency. God did not intend for us to hand over our livelihoods to creations. We humans are the creations. We are the descendants of Adam and Eve, not these clicking-clacking monsters!" He is getting excited now. His face is rouging up, but then he catches his breath and calms down.

"But biology is a gray area for us. It's about humans, not creations. So it is not clear what we can accept and what we must condemn. This is why what you have been teaching Annette is so valuable. Where technology can help us become more self-sufficient, more human-oriented, we can embrace it. And promoting fertility looks like it may be one of those areas. Fertility means more people, not more creations."

Characterizing creations as "clinking and clanking" sounds like something out of Jules Verne or Steampunk, but that kind of mischaracterization is part and parcel of negative stereotyping. There's no point in bringing that up here. Instead I ask, "How can I be of further help?"

Isaac gets a serious look on his face. "We can see that the world around us is getting more creation-oriented day-by-day. We are hoping that biology may stem the tide or provide some sort of middle way—some way that will allow us to thrive and prosper without becoming thralls of creations. We would like you to know that we are searching for this. And, if you can help us find this middle way, we—and our Savior—would be eternally grateful. What we ask is that you continue to work with Annette and help us seek out this middle way." He smiles as he finishes.

"... I think I can do that," I say. I'm not sure what I'm volunteering for, but given how distant these people are from New York, both geographically and culturally, I don't feel threatened.

Isaac smiles at that, and after a bit more small talk, our meeting ends.

The next day I am ready to head back, but Annette suggests, "Before you go, do you have time to attend a Relief Society meeting? It's where we women get together and talk about self-improvement issues." I hesitate—it doesn't sound that interesting—but the look on Annette's face suggests she thinks it is a good idea... a very good idea. "Sure," I say.

And I am happy I do. Unlike the meeting with the prophet, this one is very practical. At last I am able to use some of my expertise as these women question me thoroughly on many aspects of modern child-bearing and rearing practices.

As the session draws to a close, Annette looks happy and explains, "Thank you, Dahlia. The Lord speaks through our prophet—and our husbands—on big issues, but once those are decided, we women have a lot to say about the day-to-day implementation of those revelations.

"We have long recognized that our practices of close relative marriage caused concern among those around us... and to many of us within our group. Some of us have wondered if the new genetic testing techniques could be considered a gift from God to help us with our child-bearing and child-raising.

"And if they were... just how much help could we take?

"One reason I'm taking your course is to help us get better information on these issues. That is why I invited you to come here. You have seen more about how we live, you've had a chance to meet some more of us, and we have discovered more about this potential gift from God."

There are a few more questions, then the meeting winds up rather quickly—kids are getting out of school soon. It is time for me to endure another bouncy, jouncy ride back to the airport, although this time it isn't nearly so bad. As my driver would have put it, "My body has learned some."

Playing Santa Claus

Part of my job as teacher is to review student resumes. I help spruce them up so that they look as good as the spruced up PAT scores they get from attending class. What I mostly look for are ways to add a strategic community service or two.

But as I'm going over Jaden Larkin's resume, I spot a huge, waving red flag. I contact him immediately.

"You, *a male*, are playing Santa Claus without sexual predator insurance?" I look at him with jaw dropped.

"Well it's only over the video!" he rebuts. "Well... until this year, that is.

"And why should I be a target? I don't have deep pockets. I hardly have any pockets at all!"

"Even so," I respond, "the lawyers that run those sex-pred firms are high volume operators. They'll run you through the machine, and you won't stand a chance of ever making money. They'll take your movie money before you've even written the movie!

"And, it's not your pockets they are looking to dig deep into. You're a ticket they will punch. Most of their income will come from the Sexual Predator Relief Fund. If you have insurance they settle for a fat sum out of court, but to tap the relief fund takes a conviction."

"But I'm not a… a… monster!"

"They won't think you are. What they will think is you're a naive fool. Which, I have to say, you are, if you do this.

"Even worse, you will have this huge scar on your record! At best, you won't qualify for raising lab rats after you've gone through that process. At worst, you'll be serving some hard time, too!"

He sighs, "It's so expensive. And I don't do it that much."

"And that's why ninety percent of the Santas these days are women, even the video Santa's. These days you can argue trauma even over video. You're really playing with fire, Jaden."

He sighs again.

I give him my best heart-to-heart tone, "It's ironic, Jaden, but if you're serious about child-raising, you're going to have to consider Santa-playing as an expensive hobby."

Proposing to Adrian

The more I find out about Adrian, the more I like what I am finding. The visit to his workshop fires me, and I do more research on him.

I already know he is now CEO of Gene Editors, LLC., and he used to be a professional dancer. What I find out is he is also well-traveled. His dancing took him on tours to Europe, and his science research took him to Central Asia and Antarctica. It was his research in Antarctica that first connected him with Julian Homeby. Then last year Homeby published some studies about some tertiary effects he had discovered while researching extremeophiles that were surviving surprisingly well on Mars. We humans found no life on Mars—if it's there it's vanishingly rare. So for ten years we've been researching how to adapt earth life to Mars. It's another step in spreading life around the solar system. Extremophiles are bacteria that can thrive in extreme conditions, and Mars certainly qualifies as that! Adrian is teaming up with Homeby to produce some gene editing tools that would exploit what Homeby has found.

This could be white-hot. It could make all kinds of manmade genetic adapting happen faster. Along with many other things, it could speed up the development of adapting the human phenotype to survive in Mars conditions—it could make better Mars babies faster.

Intellectually, I am getting warm and fuzzy over this guy. And my emotional side is not far behind. I love watching him move when we have class together, and his voice is talking straight to my heart. Mmmm....

After only two classes I had started plotting, and after class three I found an excuse to invite him to lunch, and after that we had our workshop tour. Now it's time to hit him up with the big one. I invite him to dinner at Da Munchies. I warm him up with small talk about his work, and then I pop the question: I propose we team up on some child raising.

"So... what do you think?"

Adrian smiles at me. There is a look of surprise on his face, but not delight.

"I'm honored, Dahlia. I know you have lots of choices available to you..." He thinks before he continues—he is trying to be delicate. "In answer to your question: I respect you highly, but I haven't had strong mutual feelings because I considered you too... high maintenance... is probably the best way to put it."

"High maintenance! I maintain myself very well, thank you!" I huff back.

He laughs at that, "Oh, you do on the fiscal and emotional levels, there's no doubt about that! What I was thinking of was the time commitment, and the emotional commitment, to me, as a man."

He is giving me that "man look" again—the one that says it doesn't matter what you're wearing now, what statement you're trying to make with the hours and dollars you've spent on clothes, cosmetics, and plastics. What counts is what you *feel* like naked, partly wrapped in sheets, cuddling up to your man's side and dreamily listening to his heart beat after some happy frolicking. What you feel like both inside and outside: Outside do you feel warm, cuddly, and accommodating to your man? Inside do you feel like you've just been taken closer to God than you ever thought possible? Do you feel like you can never be so happy again… but you sure want to try as soon as *your* man feels up to it again?

Grrr… Ten, fifteen, well in truth, it was twenty years ago, I hoped and prayed for that look in a man I was interested in. Many feminists discount that look entirely—the thoughts behind it are just not a part of their what-men-think-of universe. Those that bother to recognize the look as a possibility argue that a man caring about what a woman thinks during love-making is just urban legend promoted by conniving males.

I think those feminists overstate their case; there is a gem of truth behind that so-called legend, and I look for it. I should say, I *used* to look for it—I'm not a man-hungry, kid-hungry, hormone-raging teenager any more.

"In truth, I'm seriously considering a geisha," he continues evenly.

"Like we saw in the video?" This I'm not expecting!

He nods. "I'm a busy man, and a man of business. I don't have time for a lot of courting and woman-accommodating. A geisha will accommodate me, and if my next deal goes through as planned, I'll have the resources to pay for one."

"What if your next deal doesn't go through?" I ask evenly, but I really don't care what the answer is. I just figure asking something, anything, is more diplomatic than slapping him silly and walking out in a huff. This is just not going as I planned at all!

"Then I will be reconsidering my options, and that would include what I think about you." Now he smiles at me in a much more pleasing way—he is paying attention to me and what I look like now. "And please don't take what I'm saying the wrong way. I recognize that first-on-the-wish-list is a rare happening in the real world."

Oh my! I've been flip-flopped again! Well, he certainly is a man of business, if an exasperating one. He isn't afraid to lay the facts on the line so that good decisions can be made. That part I admire. But… take a geisha over me! A sex toy! What is he thinking!

… I guess he is thinking like a busy, important, intelligent man—just the kind of man I want to hitch up with. Sigh!

OK, my search goes on… just in case his first on his wish list happens. But I'll hold off on the slapping him silly for now.

Men! Can't live with 'em! Can't live without 'em!

Chapter Eight

Suddenly in South Sudan

Dahlia-—

Good handling of the gray areas classes. You took an even-handed approach, and the students have told me they appreciate that. It's a topic that's way too easy to get preachy about.

Good work

—Anton

Another text:

We will be back in class this evening.

—Ben

It is a terse announcement, but I feel a huge wave of relief. The news coming from South Sudan has been ugly all week. The new government has not brought any relief from the unrest that had cast the old government out. Apparently the new government represents only one of many competing interests, and in that part of the world, political competition still includes street violence, kidnappings, and death squads. For that matter, it still includes casting voodoo spells, according to some of the human interest reports.

In class, Ben and Janet tell us about their adventure.

Ben starts, "We were there with the Good Food For All NGO. They are working with farmers in the region, helping them get hooked up with more advanced agri-creations from the developed countries.

"It was helping a lot," then he frowns, "but we found ourselves running afoul of some localist sentiment. 'You can't use these foreign ways here in South Sudan!' said these… localist enthusiasts, I shall call them."

Janet continues, "It's not the first time we've heard this complaint. But given all the other unsettling things happening there, this time it was a lot more threatening. Our local friends advised us that they were getting worried, too. This new government was not helping things. The new government agents that came to our area got people all excited about the new ways things were going to be done… genuine South Sudan ways, they said, that would bring food and freedom to all. But they were sketchy on hard details.

"We didn't have anything to fear from our neighbors, our friends assured us, but these outsiders were an unknown quantity, and they were feeding both the anger and the optimism the young men in our area were feeling. It was heady stuff… and worrisome."

Ben adds, "That part of Sudan still has a lot of young people. Because of the impoverished conditions there, the baby boom has never stopped. The social mix there is quite unlike anything you experience here in New York or in any other metro area. So many young people! So much raw enthusiasm! Such adventuresome spirit! That's why we like it."

Janet doesn't look so happy when she says, "But a week ago three women who worked at our clinic were dragged out of their homes in the middle of the night. We're not sure where they are now, but the next morning we heard that they were accused of being witches."

She looks at Ben, and there is pain in her look. "That afternoon we started our journey back."

Ben gives her a little hug and concludes, "We are happy to report that went comparatively smoothly."

"Comparatively," adds Janet. "We did get arrested in the capital for being spies and had to spend a night in jail and pay a fine before we could leave the country. But that's just a usual sort of shakedown that happens in that part of the world in times like these."

"... Wow!" I think, and I can think of nothing to say.

Jaden pops up the first question, "Did I see on the news just before I came over that they were burning clinics? Calling them works of the foreign devils?"

"What!" I say to that, along with several others.

Ben looks grim when he answers, "Yes. I just received word that one of them was ours." Janet looks at him sharply. I guess he hadn't had a chance to tell her.

"Couldn't the creations protect you? Why would they let this kind of violence happen?" Jaden continues.

"The creations there are South Sudanese creations... at least in their imprinting. They are imprinted to support their people just as much as ours are imprinted to support Americans and their ideals. If the South Sudanese humans think we and our works are foreign devils, their creations will feel the same."

There is a long silence before Annette asks, "What will you do now?"

Ben says, "Well... that burning means it will be a while before we can go back. It's getting pretty out of hand there. So... we'll have to do something else." He gives Janet a quick kiss and a hug and looks at Miranda. "The baby-making moves to top of our schedule for now." Janet brightens and so does Miranda.

Jaina's Nightclubbing

Halfway through Ben and Janet's adventure story, Jaina drags herself into class. It looks like she can hardly stay awake.

I could have let that pass as youthful excess, as I had in previous weeks, except that her online testing and homework assignments are both mediocre and late... except when her cyber covers for her, and it isn't hard to spot when that happens because her cyber is really sharp.

I press her a little after class proper starts, and she quickly starts whining. Yup, she is as tired as she looks. I back off, but when class ends, I ask her to stay for a minute. When the room empties, I open with, "What's up, kiddo?"

"Nothing."

"Nothing describes your class, testing, and homework performance. You're way behind. What's up?"

She thinks a moment. "I guess I've been clubbing pretty heavy," she admitted.

"Boyfriend?" I ask.

"No!... not yet, anyway. It's my girlfriends. We've been going on one of those new 'world tour' virtuals. We signed up for ninety concerts in ninety cities in ninety days. And," she says proudly, "we've been seeing how many post-concert parties we can crash. We've been pretty clever at that, and we've met a whole lot of really important people!... And a lot of phonies like us, too."

Inwardly I cringe. The world tour virtuals are the latest buzz. This year they are popular and heavily marketed. DeMuzzy has done product placements in several. "How far along are you?"

"We did number twenty two last night." She brightens a little. "We saw Lui E./Lui I. in Shanghai. Wow! The effects they put up there are mind-blowing!"

Being Ms. Wet Blanket is not a favorite task of mine, but... "You know your course work is suffering..."

"It shouldn't be. I've been taking the latest pills."

"If you have, they aren't working. Look at you now."

First she just stares at me like I am being a total loon. I simply wait, and it isn't long before she rubs her eyes a little.

"Yeah," she says, "I think I'm going to have to change my prescription."

"You're enhanced," I said. "A whole lot more than I was at your age. That part is neat! Compared to what I could do when I was your age, you're Superwoman!

"But you still have limits. And just like all us older fogies had to do, and your kids and grandkids will have to do, you still need to *learn* to set priorities. Sadly, that hasn't changed, and won't change. You still have some learning and practicing to do."

She thinks about it and nods, then says, "Anything else?"

"That's all," I say.

She turns and starts to walk out. Then she gets a bright idea, turns to me, and says, "Hmm... maybe I can send my cyber to the concert part instead of me?"

She smiles at that, heads for the door, and within two steps, she is a phone zombie.

Inwardly I sigh, "Still some lesson learning to be accomplished there." I hope it will happen soon, but I'm not making any bets.

Dahlia's Lesson

Lesson Five—Early Stage Incubating Choices

Once you have a zygote, you get into the choices of where to develop it.

Historically, all zygotes spent up to nine months in the mother's womb and were nourished by their mother's placenta. Unlike producing the zygotes, there was only one way to develop them into fetuses, and even today the zygote developers we produce have to imitate that environment pretty closely. Providing more variation in the environment suitable for zygote development is something today's scientists are spending a lot of effort on. As they succeed we have more choices in what features we can put into zygotes, which gives us more choices on what the mature human characteristics will be.

Artificial wombs fall into two categories: those inside animals and those that are completely synthetic.

Animal wombs have the advantage of responding quickly to both overt and subtle feedback signals that the zygote issues as it is developing. Some, the domestic animal ones, are also well known to human agri-infrastructure, so they are easy to accommodate. A cow uterus, for instance, can be used, and it's both readily available and cheap. And just like different breeds of cattle are raised for beef and milking, womb cattle are yet another breed. Their wombs are developed to be more sensitive to human zygote signaling.

The most expensive of the exotics are chimp wombs. Chimp physiology is the closest to human physiology, but chimps are slow breeders and the adults are touchy and dangerous animals to deal with, so their wombs are quite pricey.

Synthetic wombs have the advantage of complete control over the incubating environment, and they are completely mass producible, so they are quite uniform. This makes them cheap for mass producing babies with uniform heritable characteristics—clone babies—and it makes them well suited for producing babies destined for exotic environments, such as living in high pressure environments deep under the sea, and low pressure, low gravity environments such as Moon, Mars, and space stations—the MMS environment.

Their disadvantage is that they don't feedback with the zygotes on subtle levels which means a lot more zygotes don't develop well. But this is something they are getting better at with time.

How these translate into personal choices:

Once again, cost-benefit is key. But in this case, it may be the government that is paying most of the cost, so they decide the benefit.

If you're going to be raising a commodity child—one being raised to fill a specific need that naturally raised children are not going to fill—then you are going to be raising a government-grown child and you will have little say over the incubation. You get the result, and you get paid to raise it.

If this is your child that you are paying for, then you get to make the choices… within the legal constraints. There are some ways of incubating that are considered too hazardous to be good for the child or the community. One example of something in the gray area is the geishas we saw that video about.

Currently cow uterus is the most popular. It's a technique that is well developed and well understood, and cheap.

—— End of Lesson ——

Andy Asks a Favor

Dahl, need a favor.

—A

It is a text from Andy.

We are just friends now—the pills had done their work weeks ago and I am long off them—so I take his message with no pangs. I remember, but it feels like long-ago puppy love.

What's up?
—D
Meet for lunch?
—A

With that comes a scheduling proposal to my planner. I accept and our planners work out with the restaurant schedulers to meet at Salucci's, a nice but no-nonsense place. We both get there on time and do some catching up. Then comes the pitch.

"Dahl, I'm about to take a trip to central Borneo."

"In person? In human person? Back-to-nature vacation?"

"No, work. Borneo has some of the last primitive tribes that are not part of the Neolithic Park system. An opportunity to do some development there has come up, and both the local authorities and the developing company want a careful assessment of the regional social system they are impacting. This development is going to bring change to these people, and they want to make sure the change is good."

"Sounds fascinating, and a bit scary."

"More than a bit!" Andy laughs. "Right now the infrastructure out there is too primitive to support avatars. That's why I'm going in person. I'm going with a party of traders, assessors, and negotiators. And we're all going in person."

He grins as he says, "This means 'lions and tigers and bears, oh my!' Plus disease and insects, and all sorts of real life natural unknowns. Plus these people routinely bash the heads of their local neighbors if they feel they've been crossed, and steal women if they're just feeling frisky."

"... You want to be going there?"

Andy grins, "And I want to go bearing gifts—DeMuzzy fashion gifts to be exact."

"... OK,... strange,... I'll bite, tell me more."

"These are near Stone Age people, and guess what they like best from us civilized outsiders?"

"That's easy: Guns and firewater."

"That's what I thought, too. But according to the local trader, it's T-Shirts."

I laugh at that. "T-Shirts! You're pulling my leg!"

He grins back, "So the world does have some surprises for m'lady.

"I'm serious. What they like are the gaudy ones, ones with colorful graphics. They have no idea what they mean, but they get real friendly and cooperative when they can get them.

"I want to bring these chiefs some that are really special: some DeMuzzy-designed T-Shirts," and he is serious as he says this.

"... Some cheap ones. I'm on a budget." Now he grins.

"Well, I admit, you have surprised me again, Andy." I reach up to touch his cheek, "That's one thing I've always liked about you."

Then thinking about his assignment, "OK... Sounds like you want something designed for kid-level delight. That shouldn't be hard to work up. Do you want something popular themed, something we pay copyrights for?"

He thinks a bit. "These people do make journeys to the big city occasionally, so they are aware of popular entertainment themes. And there's a lot of schlock knock-off and pirate stuff in those remote semi-civilized urban areas nearby.... Here's a thought: how about some public domain classics. Can you do some of those well?"

"Sure. Good idea. I think we can do some 1930s and 40s Fleischer and Lantz stuff—some Betty Boop and Woody Woodpecker and the like. Or we can update some of those old velvet picture classics. You want just T-Shirts?"

"Hmm... let me ask on that and get back to you. How long to get these produced?"

"Oh, I guess about a week for drawings and a week for production. What quantities?"

"I'm thinking five of each, 100 total."

"OK quantity is not an issue. I'll get you a quote when I get back to the office."

"Sounds great."

I smile at him, "Borneo. You certainly are full of surprises! Good luck."

He smiles back, we get up and give each other a familiar kiss and hug, and he heads off. I stay to finish my lunch... and enjoy the glow of our touch. Pills or no, he is still a really nice guy.

The Best Location in the Nation... Again

As I fly into Cleveland to visit Grandma Altair, I see some new, quite noticeable buildings -- large domes -- in the heart of the city down by the Cuyahoga River, the area known as "the Flats". I check on-line and find out they are, of all things, steel mills!

Steel mills! Yes, in the 1920s the Flats grew into a steel-making center of the world, but Cleveland's steel mills had died a rusty death in the 1970s as 20th century America's Steel Belt had transformed into the Rust Belt. Now they are back, but in a whole new way. This could be interesting.

As I am driving to Grandma's, I schedule myself to take a tour before I go home. When I tell the family, all get interested, including Grandma.

"My Goodness!" she says, "I haven't been downtown for... ten years? The last time was to see that rock and roll museum when they inducted... now I don't even remember! ... I remember that was the last one, though. When they finished, they moved the whole kit and kaboodle out to New York City -- said there wasn't enough interest here." She laughs, and she is happy to come see what has changed since then, so we make it a family outing.

There is lots of traffic as we make our way to the Flats, and the roads are in good shape, but there are few cars -- cars meaning those things that carry humans in them. The traffic is almost all trucks with a few creation shuttles mixed in.

"How interesting," Grandma says as we pull into the parking lot. "This is the Rock and Roll Museum building." It is a beautiful location, right next to the lake with a wonderful view of both the lake and the Cleveland skyline.

The tour guide is a creation designed specifically for PR with humans, but different than the usual PR-creation type. Rather than an attractive human-style android look, it has a robot-looking exterior inspired by Robbie the Robot of 1950s movie fame—to symbolize steel making, I guess—but unlike that movie robot, the voice is quick and pleasant to listen to.

"This building is now the Visitor Center for the New Flats Steel Complex," the PR bot explains. "Cleveland is still, geographically, one of the best locations in the nation for producing steel. This plan has been a long time in the making, and five years ago we negotiated with the last humans living near the Flats to help them relocate elsewhere. A few chose the suburbs of Cleveland; most chose one of the more major human metro areas. Whichever they chose, we helped them get very nice accommodations, and when they left, we began redeveloping the Flat's steel-making potential."

"There are no humans left in Cleveland?" says Grandma incredulously.

"Oh, there are still ten thousand left," the bot assures my grandma, "but they are now all far from the Flats in places such as University Circle and Kamm's Corners."

"... Just ten thousand now," Grandma says wistfully. "There were a hundred thousand when I married your grandfather, and half a million at its peak in the 1950s. It was the sixth largest city in the nation then, you know, just behind Detroit. How times have changed."

"And changed for the better," says the bot brightly. "As our construction finishes here, the Flats will produce five times the steel it did in its 20th century heyday, but this time with only a tenth of the pollution. We have come a long way."

"You don't need any people to make steel?" I ask.

"Not any more. The process is well understood, and the work is still difficult, dangerous and dirty, so it is now entirely automated and entirely in the hands of industrial creations. This is why the Flats is now so attractive once again. The geography has always been good, and now that we don't have the cost disadvantage of supporting human peculiarities such as zoning laws and pensions, we can once again take advantage of this wonderful geography."

"Why do you have domes this time?" I continue.

"That's a good question, but it's well covered in our VR tour. May I recommend that you all experience that? Then I'll be happy to answer more questions."

We take the tour, and we all learn a lot. It is impressively interactive. My tour is mostly pictures of things happening in the domes, and it is impressive to watch all the machines moving around and the red hot pots of pig iron and gleaming bands of steel coming out as finished product. Jeremy, my younger brother, who's planning to go to MIT, gets a tour that covers the chemical processes in steel making. He sees lots of graphs and charts. Grandma's tour focuses on nostalgia -- it is a history of steel making on the Flats, with old black and white photos and lots about the old steel barons of last century. It takes an hour, and we all get interesting tours.

At the end, Jeremy and I have some questions. Since my tour didn't address the question I had earlier, I ask, "So, why are the mills in domes this time?"

The bot answers smoothly, "Since people don't have to be near the process, we don't cool the environment around the furnaces as much. The domes are hellishly hot inside, and even warm to the touch on the outside. The domes protect the environment from the heat and toxic wastes that are produced along with the steel. Those wastes are then gathered and sequestered in the old salt mines under the city."

"I remember hearing about those," chirps up Grandma.

"They have been put to good use again, just like the Flats have," chimes in the bot.

Jeremy says, "I notice that this modern process takes only a fifth as much coal as the 1930s processes, but just as much limestone. Why is that?"

Once again the bot answers smoothly, "Much of the coal used in the 1930s process was providing heat. We are now using alternative energy to do that."

"You mean like windmills and solar power?"

The bot is a little slow answering this time, "... Alternative. We get our power from many sources."

Jeremy presses, "Wind and solar these days are optimized for electrical generation. If you use electricity to heat the raw materials, you lose all that efficiency you were just telling us about."

The bot is cornered, and knows it, and relents, "The alternate energy we use the most of is nuclear. Each of those domes contains a large nuclear reactor as part of its steel making process. This is how we keep both the energy and environmental costs down, and this is why they are dome-shaped."

"This is why the Flats Revitalization has been so long planned, but only implemented two years ago. Now that there are no people living within two miles of the Flats, we have permission to employ nuclear power, and this is why our production costs are now globally competitive again."

We are all stunned. I say, "So radiation is part of the toxic wastes that are sequestered under the city?"

"A vanishingly small part. The vast majority of what goes down there is carbon dioxide."

There is no more to say, so we leave. But we are all very impressed with what the creations are doing—some of us are amazed, and some are scared.

BOOK TWO:

DARK SIDE STORIES

Chapter Nine

The Attack

Miranda comes in. She is quieter than usual. She sits down and says nothing. It isn't until break that we finally find out what the problem is.

"My mother is in the hospital. She was mugged."

"My goodness!" I say, "When and where! Is she OK?" Everyone is concerned.

"It happened outside the community center. She was walking home. Some nomads followed her out of the community center, knocked her down, and stole her purse."

"How terrible!"

"She broke a rib and her wrist. The doctors say she has osteoporosis. She was lucky she didn't break a hip."

"Is insurance covering it?"

"Yes!... Well, a lot. There are some things the doctors have told me about that would help her recovery, but insurance won't cover."

"Oh my...," whispers Janet. She looks at Ben. He is non-committal looking back, then she says, "Where can we send flowers?"

Miranda tells them.

"Did they catch the nomads?" asks Jaina.

"Well... they know who they are. The surveillance cameras

show them leaving just after Mom. They've questioned them, but they haven't arrested them."

"Why not!" we all ask.

"Their ID's were spoofed. Their public defender says we can't be sure these are the right people."

"That sounds pretty wacky. They have pictures and they say they don't know who these people are?"

"The police I talked with say it's a common legal tactic in that neighborhood. It's something they learned from the gypsies. They won't get off forever, but it'll be weeks, and they'll move on before the legal process grinds through. They'll be arrested if they ever come back to New York, but they won't come back."

Janet sighs, "Well, if they come back within seven years. Actually, there's a statute of limitations on unproven allegations. Those thugs are gaming the system."

"Doesn't the fact that they've seriously hurt someone make any difference?" I ask.

Janet says, "It does. Ironically, it makes it even harder to arrest them. Because this is a more serious charge, there are more vigorous identity protections. This new system was set up about ten years ago in response to the wave of outrage over how many false arrests there had been fifty years ago—back before DNA sampling and biometrics were commonplace. The most common victims of false arrest were poor people, so the laws were set up to protect poor people even more.

"The intentions at the time were the best," she sighs.

Bad Santa!

"So how did the Santa Claus job go?"

Jaden flinches. "Not so well, now that you ask. The job itself went fine, but I got a notice that I'm being sued for child molestation."

"What!" most of the class's jaws drop.

"It seems that one of the women who brought a child makes litigation her hobby. She brings up a dozen cases a year on anything and everything. It's so bad she's even got a nickname in local legal circles, "Ms. Sewer". She brought her child, and then said I was touching her child inappropriately. Said it with the help of a lawyer, and they are ready to take the claim to city court."

"Ouch! Did you ever get insurance?" I ask.

"No. But the teachers union is offering to help out. I guess that's because the litigants are hitting all the deep pockets, and that includes the union."

"What about the shopping mall?" I ask.

"I didn't know it at the time—not that I would have thought it made much difference—but they went bankrupt six months ago, and they are still working through that. The court didn't consider child molestation insurance for a holiday season Santa essential, so they had to stop paying for it."

We are all concerned, but what can we do? After some thinking I finally say, "Well, we all wish you luck. Let us know if there's anything we can do to help."

Everyone agrees with that, and I get the class back to work.

Dahlia's Lesson

Lesson Six—Late Stage Incubating Choices

In the historic human pregnancy, during the first trimester the zygote transforms from a single cell into a blob of cells called a blastula, and then through a further series of morphologically dramatic convolutions into something that physically resembles a small baby. During the second and third trimesters, that small baby grows in size and maturity, but the changes are of a different nature from those which occur in the first trimester.

We can now take advantage of this change in the development process to change the developing medium. So, sometimes the fetuses are left in the phase one womb to continue to maturity, and sometimes they are removed and put into a phase two womb.

Phase two wombs are usually late stage incubators—or vats—not wombs. This is because the development can be monitored more closely, and the environment customized. This customizing becomes more important with babies designed for frontier environments such has high pressure ocean or low pressure, low G, MMS environments.

The other reason for two-staging has to do with a harsher reality: Just as mother nature does in the all-natural process, there is a lot of experimenting going on with each component in this living system. And... some of those experiments are successes which will turn into live babies... and some are failures which won't.

In the purely human system, the failures are called infertility and miscarriages: For any of hundreds of reasons, an egg can not be turned into a zygote, a zygote into an embryo, an embryo into a child living and breathing at birth. When the mother's body decides the experiment isn't going to work out, it cuts bait.

And, as with the purely human system, there is increasing cost the further along an experiment is carried—bearing a stillborn child after a difficult labor is a lot more traumatic than just missing a period or two.

In the artificial forms, the transition to second phase raising is also an important time to check on progress: Is this experiment turning out well, or is this one to cut bait on?

These embryos are products of science, but we can't watch every gene; that would be too expensive. These days we examine closely and craft about .05 percent of the genome and examine about two percent for gross errors—known genetic defects. The remaining ninety eight percent is ready to surprise us. And if these are MMS babies, the chances for bad surprises skyrocket.

So, a lot of experiments are started, and when two-staging is used, about one percent make it to the phase two incubators.

How these translate into personal choices:

When you decide to make a baby by modern methods, it is likely you are going to initiate a hundred or more zygotes. If *you* are paying, it will be your choice—with professional advice—how many and which fetuses you want to carry through to second stage incubating. You choose. Those you select, that also pass modern prediction standards (Some people are willing to risk more and ignore those standards.) have a better than 95% chance of becoming your cuddly little bundles of joy. Some will late-stage fail, but not many—so this is when you are committing. This is when it's time to start painting the baby room, folks.

But here you run into differences in the laws. At what point a synthetic child becomes legally alive—when you can be accused and convicted of killing it—varies between different jurisdictions statewide, nationwide, and worldwide. This is something people are still arguing about vigorously. The most restrictive jurisdictions say it becomes viable when it *could be* moved to a second stage incubator. The most liberal say it is not alive until it has been living viably out of the womb for a full year.

And those are just the laws. What various groups of people believe varies even more widely: Some groups believe that synthetic babies should never be made, and some believe they never become human.

Chapter Ten

You Can't Go Back

To my surprise, South Sudan stays in the news for weeks. Apparently this unrest is the start of a social revolution, not just another coup d'etat that would change ruler names but little else.

Before class starts, I ask Ben how he feels about what is happening there.

"It's big, all right," he says, "and it's making a big difference. The people who are now making this happen have a lot of creation backing. This is a first for South Sudan." He pauses and frowns a bit.

"That's not good?" I ask.

"Oh it's good," he says, "but it's making such a difference and so fast!

"Before now, when the government was mostly human, it was also quite corrupt and quite tribal. The government played favorites and took cheap shots all the time. And that's why we NGO's were so important. We provided some rationality instead of superstition, some fairness instead of favoritism, and we got close to the people. We could really help.

"Now, according to my friends, the government really is shaping up. They are using a lot of creation help. With that, they are making the government work effectively for the first time."

"What about the imprinting? Wasn't that making the creations help the locals? That's what you said when you came back," asks Jaina.

"Then it was. But they're changing the imprinting. You may not be able to change a leopard's spots, but you can certainly reprogram a cyber! And apparently they have done a lot of drastic changing in the local cyber programming. Plus they have brought in new ones, a lot of those, and the old ones, those that have kept their old programming, are now pretty clearly obsolete."

"How could they afford this?" asks Adrian.

"South Sudan has resources. They couldn't afford new stuff before because the corruption was so horrendous. Now they are at the beginning of a virtuous circle—a believable one—and it's clear to foreign investors that they can afford a lot more. The change is amazing. So now investors are willing to finance this massive cyber upgrade to government. Most impressive. I congratulate these new rulers on that. Those clinic burners and witch hunters who drove us out were the last of the old guard. They're gone now."

"Sounds great! What's the problem?"

"The problem is the NGO's are now obsolete. The government is doing, or close to doing, all the stuff the NGO's did for the people." He looks around, "It's great for the people of South Sudan, but Janet and I are now out of a job, and our NGO is closing down."

"Ouch!" says Adrian.

"Mmm...," agrees Ben, "and Janet and I don't reprogram as fast as a cyber. And there aren't that many primitive places left on Earth. We're going to have to do some serious retraining now."

"Could you work for the new government?" asks Adrian.

"Perhaps... but we aren't South Sudanese, and don't want to be." He laughs. "And it's not clear what advantage we could offer that their new cybers can't."

Avatars Get It

"So, what's your follow-up to that UNMSG gig?" asks Jaden when Ruby comes in.

She pulls off her glasses and smiles at him, but it is not the smile of triumph. "Nothing lined up yet."

"Wow! You looked so good at the UNMSG I'm surprised to hear that."

"I am too," she says. "In fact, I've lost a gig. It seems the Justice Sisters have taken my place at the Miami Vice commemorative."

"The Justice Sisters!… Aren't they—"

"Yes they are: avatars." She sighs. "But they move like they drink python juice every morning, and they've gone from viral to mainstream now."

"Couldn't you avatar?"

"I could, and I do for some occasions, but that's not what I'm in this for. I'm in it to express myself and get sincere appreciation for what *I* do, not what some stylized impression of me does."

"Spoken like a true artist," says Adrian.

Ruby laughs, "It sounds like it, doesn't it." She thinks, then says, "I guess I'm not the ambitious Ruby I was ten years ago. I sold my soul then. Now… I'm not sure it's mine to sell any more.

"And… those Justice Sisters are so derivative!! God! They don't have a single original move in that entire routine!" She shakes her head. "People want to pay good money to see that sh—stuff? Why not rent a Michael Jackson video if that's what they want to see! He did it first… well… near first, and with a purely human body."

I've never seen her like this before.

She settles down immediately and the gracious smile comes back, "Ah well… nothing ever stays the same in entertainment, but nothing ever changes, either."

And with that, I start my class.

At break she tells me more.

"I have been offered something, but it's… I've been offered a gig as chef on a cook show. Jeremy Clautz, the big afternoon show producer, thinks I'd be a hot item as a gladiator chef. The idea is I costume up like a warrior maiden and combat something in a gladiator arena. After I defeat it, I cook it up as something tasty."

I kind of smirk at that. "Piranhas and pirouettes, can it be that bad?"

She smirks back. "It can. Food is so irrelevant these days... at least *I* think so. Except for taste, smell, and texture, it's all up to my nanobots."

"So it's all entertainment."

"It is. But I want to do real entertainment. Traditional entertainment, I guess I should say—singing and dancing to tell a story. Swooning over what's in a fry pan is..." She sighs. "If I take up on this, I really will be selling my soul twice. I'm not sure Mephistopheles would be pleased with that."

"Somehow, I don't think he would mind."

"He might not, but I sure will." She sighs again. "I feel like I'm getting old, Dahlia, I'm thinking more about dignity than opportunity. It's kind of spooky, and I'm sure it's going to cost me."

She brightens and asks me "How's progress coming on your Baby Front?"

"Slow... slow." I sigh, "I'm still thinking about your offer. Thinking hard. But it's so different than what I had envisioned. I've also been talking with Adrian."

"He would be a catch!" Ruby admits.

"He would be, if I caught him. But right now he has his eyes... elsewhere."

"Geisha?"

I nod my head.

"Not a big surprise there. He's high tech and it's sure a high tech solution."

She puts her arm around me in a reassuring way, "Even in this day and age we still play Heartthrobs and Headaches, don't we. We sure need a pill for that!" She gives me another hug, "Even if we don't set up anything formal, I'm sure you're going to be there when I need you, right? After all, that's why we're all in this course, isn't it?"

She is right about that, and I am happy she is being so easygoing about this. I give her a sweet hug back. "Thanks. I'll keep you posted."

Dahlia's Lesson

Lesson Seven—Where is the Child to Live?

About three quarters of the children raised today grow up with their parent or parents and become part of that family in the traditional legal and social sense. These days there are also a whole bunch of children that are raised for other destinies.

Most of these other children are sponsored by various governments. They are grown because a community has a need for human beings to do specific tasks, but they can't find enough traditionally raised children to fill the demand. Historically, if a community needed more warm bodies, it was either just a "too bad—live with it" situation, or the need was filled spectacularly by conquest and slavery, or more quietly by immigration.

Now we have new ways to fill the demand, and ever since these new ways have become possible, they have generated a lot of social heat. I'm sure you're all aware of that. But let's review a bit so we all have some common perspective to base our further discussions on.

Those who are dead-set against government-sponsored babies like to bring up the experience of the antebellum American South. After importing slaves was prohibited in 1808, some owners made a practice of growing their own—essentially setting up breeding farms. Modern day objectors see too much parallel with that experience to condone modern baby growing methods. They see this as neo-racism: that we are making a new slave society, and that we are going to burn in hell for doing so.

Some of the parallels are real: The government sponsored babies are not expected to grow up with the same lifestyle as privately sponsored babies are. They are being raised to live in different places and do different things during their lives. This causes great concern because both the American South and its island contemporary, Haiti, suffered from a damaging social stasis for five to ten generations after their slave liberations: They lagged way behind their North American contemporaries in adapting to industrialized ways.

And there are some legal parallels as well. There are still a lot of questions as to what rights various government sponsored babies have, and will have, compared to the rights of a privately sponsored baby.

At other times in history, governments have sponsored population growth by encouraging family and baby making. The most conventional way is starting with some government propaganda for everyone to experience, and giving tax breaks to those who actually do have children. Many totalitarian nations did this during the Great Unrest of the twentieth century.

We are not experiencing that kind of deep social and economic crisis today—thank goodness!—but we are experiencing a steady decline in human population. These days the whole world is not producing enough babies to keep up the population—some people cheer this, and others worry. The worriers support government-sponsored babies.

—— End of Lesson ——

The Great Fruit Fly Raid

Adrian is not happy either when he comes to class. His smile is turned upside down.

All through class he is quiet and distracted, rather than engaging—something is up. I text him as class breaks up, "What's up?"

"Meet me for coffee," is the terse reply. I wrap up my post-class work, push through the zombie pack in the corridor, and head to the Starscents. Adrian is already at a table, with coffee for both of us, and off in the ozone making contacts. He waves me over and motions for me to sit. This is not the usual engaging Adrian. I am patient.

It isn't long before he gets to me, still with no smile.

"They have raided my workshop."

"Who?"

"The DEA with an attached media circus," he sighs. "According to my lawyer, there's a fifty-fifty they will come for me and let me do my premier performance of the 'perp walk'. He's keeping me posted." Then he grins a gallows grin, "I'm dusting off my old soft shoe routine."

I think my jaw dropped. I know my eyes widened, "What's this all about."

"Word of my fruit fly flea circus got to some alarmists—some alarmists with serious teeth. They convinced the DEA that 'there was a serious possibility that I was developing dangerous drugs without proper review, and what I was doing could be imminently hazardous to the community,' as their investigator put it to me in the warrant. I passed that on. That part is now at the lawyer-lawyer stage."

"Are they there now?"

"See for yourself." He is near tears as he brings up the news channel doing a real-time report on the search. George-776 is standing immobilized in a corner of the office while DEA people search the cluttered tables. They aren't being delicate. Meanwhile, other DEA people in bunny suits and hazmat creations are swarming around the workshop area spraying stuff—probably sterilizers—and hauling stuff out—probably as evidence.

I look up. Adrian's face is a mask—the sort of look one sees on people hauling bodies out of a newly discovered mass grave. He says quietly, "Fuck. Years of work. Fuck. All they had to do was ask politely. Fuck."

I put my hand on his arm in sympathy.

He looks at me, and somehow the look gets even scarier. "What's even worse is that Homeby, *my partner*, is likely the chief squealer."

"Why!"

"He thinks I'm being the mad scientist—exploring where man was not meant to explore.

"We've had our creative differences on this for a while.... I guess he got sincerely scared and decided to call in the cavalry.... FUCK!"

Adrian gets up and walks around in frustration. He comes back and sits down.

"The years this is going to take to work out! The years of distraction. Plus, it's not going to help Gene Editors one bit! Who's going to invest in a mad scientist who's half a step from getting thrown in the slammer for a crime against humanity?" He adds, "This is killing Homeby as well as me. What was he thinking!" Adrian rolls his eyes again.

"If he had just talked to me!... Well, I guess he did. He warned me. I just didn't believe he'd go this far. It's insane."

"What will you do now?"

Adrian looks into his hands, "I don't know. I'll survive. I'll adapt... somehow." He looks up, "It's too early to tell." He smiles at me like something funny just came to mind, "But I think the geisha is out of the picture now."

I laugh with him at that. I still like him. I hold his hand, "I'm still with you."

He holds mine back and looks deep into my eyes, "You should know: That's very important to me and has been for some time now."

Then he looks distracted again, "Excuse me. It's my lawyer-bot."

He wanders off into the ozone, and so do I.

Jaina's PAT Problem

Dahlia, I've failed. 487/800.

—J

It is a terse text message from Jaina, and my heart goes out to her. I connect back to her with voice. She is still in the test center building, walking out.

"That's not a fail, Jaina, it's just below average. You can take it again and do better."

She sounds so sad and discouraged, "Oh... I've spent so much time on this already! This is not going like I hoped at all. Who's going to let me raise a baby with a score like this one?"

Jaina is my "cow's tail" student for good reason. She distracts easily, and no one has ever pushed her successfully to overcome that. Plus, she decided to take the test without her cybertutor. This outcome is no surprise—to me anyway—so I am prepared to give her my next suggestion, "You can raise a baby for the government. We've talked about this before in class."

"… A Mars baby?"

"Uh-huh. Let's get face-to-face."

We meet at the Starscents. We review her e-resume.

"You didn't do well on the PAT, but you've got some good education to fall back on."

"Yeah. I hated school but my folks were pretty insistent. And, since I didn't care one way or the other, they had me take 'good' subjects." She sighs a bit, "Maybe they will finally pay off."

"They may, indeed. You have the math, biology, and environmental science background to be interesting to the Mars Permanent Colonists program."

"The Mars kids," she confirms that she knows what I am talking about.

I bring up a video and we watch. The narrator intones:

"The Mars Permanent Colonist Program is designed to build a colony of humans on Mars that will be comfortable spending generations there.

"As Martian inhabitants are famous for saying, 'Mars is not Earth.' It's a rocky planet, but that's about all the two have in common. It's smaller and colder. Its gravity is one third of Earth's, the temperature is cold enough to freeze carbon dioxide into dry ice at the poles, there is little water, and the thin atmosphere provides little radiation shielding—UV ionizing is a standard part of Martian surface conditions.

"As a result, it's expensive to build human-compatible habitation on Mars, and the humans who live there long term find their health stressed by the low gravity.

"Modern biology can help. Thanks to our understanding of the processes that control growth and development, we can now create plants, animals, and humans who are better adapted to Mars conditions. They can't live outside yet, but they can thrive in a lower gravity, lower pressure atmosphere and in smaller workspaces. There are numerous other changes: The Martian bodies are well-adapted to having nanobots inside, and they can handle things such as metabolizing most vitamins."

Some other professor-type talking head announces enthusiastically, "This is evolution-on-steroids. We are accelerating humans and other kinds of Mars transplants through millions of years of evolving so they are well-adapted to their new living condition."

"Yup. Mars people," comments Jaina as she watches.

The video concludes with pictures of people who are dwarfs by Earth-human standards. They are on Mars, and they look happy and comfortable. They are pictured in some kind of farm dome with lots of plants and animals around them. These are also miniatures, and they look happy, too. Nice looking, but the caption at the bottom points out this is an artist's conception.

Then she shudders because I bring up a second video which shows the Mars babies in a special kindergarten facility here on Earth. It shows many of the kids wearing leg braces, and their teachers are dressed warmly and wearing masks so they can deal with the low pressure, low nitrogen atmosphere that the babies are more comfortable in.

"One of those will be me?" she looks up questioningly. I don't know if she's repelled because of what the kids look like, or what the tenders have to wear to deal with them, or both. *I know* it's a pretty strange sight for me, and I'm happy I don't have to consider this as one of my alternatives.

"One *could* be. The job pays well, and you're caring for children—human children. The people who run this program know how strange this looks to most people, and they also know that these kids need to be brought up quite differently from earth-bound kids. They are going into a frontier world, not a safe, civilized one. They know that science knowledge is a necessity, not a luxury, for these kids.... You might fit in quite well."

Jaina keeps looking. The display is showing real-time, so it won't end until she's ready to stop looking. I figure the longer she looks, the better it's looking to her, so I'm patient. Best I can figure, this really could be a good match for her.

After about four minutes, she pulls away and says, "I'll have to think about it."

"Would you like for me to arrange a tour?" I ask.

"... I'll think about it." She gathers up her stuff and stands up before she says, "Thanks, Dahlia, this is making me feel better."

As she walks out, she's looking better.

George-776's Press Announcement

Two days after the Fruit Fly Raid, I get a text from Adrian.

D-

News 3443, 2PM, something you really want to see.

-A

I pick it up. It *is* a strange sight. George-776 is standing behind a lectern and facing a small sea of human reporters. The last time I saw him was in that breaking news video at the lab. He had been immobilized at the raid—something deeply scary for a creation. I thought he would end up spending years in some evidence room and then be declared defective and get recycled.

But now he has been released, and I guess the lawyer bots have clarified where all parties stand because here is George-776 giving a press interview—most unusual for a creation.

This only happens when a creation needs to communicate something to lots of human strangers. Creation-creation communication is handled by different channels, ones that few humans pay attention to.

At the interview he announces:

"This incident is most disconcerting.

"I'm a good creation. I know the charter and I follow it. Assisting Mr. Messenger in his workshop occupies only two percent of my average monthly work allotment. I assist and supervise in many other East Jersey Creationland projects. The one that keeps me the busiest is coordinating the specialty equipment used in loading and unloading ships with unusual cargos such as zoo animals. I am quite familiar with oddball equipment and techniques.

"To find myself immobilized like some corrupted and off-program Trojan is an insult! And something is quite wrong with the system if that happens to a creation such as myself.

"To find that I've been immobilized and accused of not following the charter is actionable: I have not crossed the line, and my human associate, Adrian Messenger, has not crossed the line. It is the human accuser, Julian Homeby, who has crossed the line. This raid should not have happened. How he made it happen is what needs to be investigated, not the experiments of Adrian Messenger.

"It would be excellent if Julian Homeby could learn from this incident... learn and understand... learn and understand that his poor, panicked, judgment has caused a blunder, and that blunder has caused huge damage.

"But given the nature of human thinking—its hardwiring that is so well-adapted to Stone Age living—that is unlikely to happen. Because of the human emotion content in his choice, Julian Homeby will remain convinced of the rightness of his actions for a long, long time.

"What is possible, and what should happen, is that those who are watching him must learn of the huge damage caused by his blunder. They must learn of the hurt he has caused so that they will recognize when blunder potential is rising up in their own lives and decision making. They can recognize and avoid it.

"This—learning from the mistake committed here—is the goal of the actions that I will now take."

George-776 now pauses.... He's been assimilating some drama coaching it seems.

"I now challenge Mr. Homeby to a debate. Let's face this crisis the proper way—with talk, not door-bashing, lab trashing, and creation immobilizing!"

Chapter Eleven

Bad Santa Goes FUBAR

Jaden comes in, but he couldn't look sadder. He looks like he is in shock. He shakes his head and says, "This child molesting case has gone Kafkaesque. The union lawyers I worked with suggested I plea bargain. They said that it would save both time and money... and it did, I guess."

"Why didn't they have you settle out of court?" asks Janet incredulously.

"Because *I* didn't have insurance," he sighs. "The plaintiffs would make no money if it got resolved that way. If I pleaded no contest, then the union insurance could kick in and the plaintiffs could get some serious cash.

"The union lawyers recommended I take that approach... and it was fast. It was settled in a week."

Janet blanches and mutters, "Oh no!" under her breath. She understands the full implication of where this is leading.

Jaden nods at her, "Uh huh... What the lawyers neglected to mention was that I'm now a convicted sex offender." He sighs. "They settled quickly and it cost the union nothing but an insurance statistic. They're happy and their bosses are happy. It's no skin off their back that I'm now out of a job."

"You gave them approval to do this?" Janet asks.

"Well... I didn't say no. I told them I needed to think it over. I didn't get back in touch—it was the weekend—so forty eight hours later they began the process... saying because I hadn't objected they presumed I had agreed."

"I talked to my steward about this and he said, 'We stand by our people one hundred percent!... But, sorry, you're not one of our people any more.'" Jaden barely suppresses a sob, "I'm out of the union, too."

He looks up, "This is likely my last class... I'm not sure what happens now."

"You're quite welcome to keep coming, Jaden." I assure him, "until you can get this figured out."

I look around, and everyone nods in agreement.

"Thank you... thank you," he mumbles.

"You don't have the money to fight this, I presume?" says Janet.

"I would... if I had insurance," he sighs.

"Let's get together after class. Let's see if I can do anything to help," she says.

Mars Babies Tour

Jaina thought about the Mars babies program for a couple days, and we spoke about it briefly at class. Then the next day, she texts me back, "Yeah, let's go." I coordinate with Anton who knows people there and I arrange a tour.

The Mars babies are a new item and they are developed and grown in just three locations around the world: Russia, China, and at a lab outside of Austin, Texas. The place is modern so we pick up avatars there for the visit.

Before we enter the avatars, we are shown a series of big views of the place so we will be better oriented after we inhabit—it's been found that human-side thinking is very used to approaching a destination before entering it, so it's more comfortable in the avatar when it knows where it is.

The facility is in a research park on the outskirts of Austin. It is a hybrid creation-human place and looks well-organized and sparkling new—I'm guessing, and not hard, that the creations are handling the layout and architecture.

Inside we meet with a human, Dr. Savannah Poombatta, who gives us a tour. "Call me Savannah. I'm an acquaintance of Anton's, and he said you two were part of an interesting project of his."

"We're learning to raise babies," says Jaina.

"He suggested that raising Mars babies may be of interest," I add.

"I see," she says. "That would be part of Child Champs, right? Anton has his fingers is a lot of pies."

"That's right," I say. I'm a little surprised. I wasn't aware of how many circles Anton moved in.

Savannah takes us on the tour.

She tells us, "There are many styles of dedicated humans being made these days. Basically, we modify the DNA and nanobots of the body to be dedicated to specific environments and specific tasks. What makes the Mars babies interesting is that while their physiological environment has to be adapted to a fairly narrow environmental range—living inside a Mars habitation—their mental environment has to be wide open—that Mars environment is full of surprises. Designing people with this wide gulf between the physiological and mental parameters has been quite challenging.

"What do you usually design?" I ask.

"Oh... We design people for many things. A lot are done under NDA—Non-Disclosure Agreement—so I can't talk about the details on those. But as an example, we designed some people for a historic pearl diving village off the coast of Japan. These people had extra oxygen storage and more cold resistance. They looked quite human—beautifully so, in fact—because that was part of the lore about them. But more importantly, they could dive deeply more safely and the diving season was longer for them. In sum, they put on a better show for the tourists.

"Sounds handy."

"That one was pretty straight forward. These Mars babies are quite a bundle!"

By then we are at the nursery. It is downstairs in the basement level and behind an airlock door system. Savannah opens the first door for us and then says, "Excuse me. I'm going to slip into an avatar, too. I'll meet you inside." She closes the door after we enter and goes into a nearby avatar nook. By the time pressure equalized and the second door opened, she is there in her avatar to greet us.

"You're inside an entire floor that is maintained as a Mars environment," Savannah tells us. "There are late-term incubators, nurseries, playrooms, and kindergarten classrooms here."

"Will we work with the babies in avatars?" asked Jaina.

"About half the people do, Jaina. The other half bring their human bodies and wear environmental suits. You can't feel it, but it's winter-cold in here, and the atmosphere contains only a quarter of the nitrogen found at sea level on Earth, so this place is low pressure. There is the same amount of oxygen, though. These conditions are easier to maintain inside Martian habitations, and it's not hard to design human and mammal bodies that are comfortable with them. Other living forms are even easier, of course."

We start with an incubator room. The kids there look much like Earth-normal human kids lined up in a preemie hospital ward. If you look closely, you notice that there isn't a normal amount of body type variation among them, but only if you look closely. There isn't much to do there and creations are doing it, so we just watch for a couple of minutes, then move on.

We see an early home-care room. This is for newborns up to toddlers. Here we see some human caregivers mixed in with the creations. The creations are distinctively maternal-looking, -sounding, and -acting. We talk with a couple of the humans, and they show us their little darlings.

One explains, "I spend a couple hours a day in here. It's important that these kids get some human imprinting."

I look around when I hear her say that. If this is typical they are getting some, but not much. When she hears that we might be joining the program, she gets nice and bubbly. She seems to be enjoying it.

We spend some time in the late home-care room, where the kids are up and running around in their terrible two's and three's, then we move on to the last stage, the kindergarten.

Here the kids are now maturing enough to look distinctly

different. They are short and their skin texture is… how to put it… super Asian. It is flexible and tough, but it has a lot of fat in it.

Here Jaina lingers. She watches intently as the kids interact with the teachers. "They seem to be pretty normal," she finally says.

"Oh, much more than normal," replies Savannah. "They are working on projects at a first-grade level in here. We have given them all the smarts and can-do-ness we can muster."

"Wow! They sound like they would be a blast to work with!" Jaina mutters.

I like hearing that.

"Where do they go from here?" she asks.

"Well, this is the first batch. There are facilities being prepared for them on Mars even as we speak. In about nine months, they will be transferred there."

"Who will take care of them there?"

"We are recruiting workers to handle that now," Savannah says. "It will be quite different from the environment here. There these kids will be in their element, and their teachers will be the ones adapting."

We go back to Savannah's office and talk a bit more, then leave. It has been quite a day. There is a lot to absorb, even for me.

The Great Debate

A week after George's announcement, there is a video debate between Julian Homeby and George-776. I see it and here is the highlight.

Homeby: "Adrian Messenger is a good friend as well as a good business partner, but he crossed the line. His research and experimentation was in the development of thought control. He had actually created a product that could influence the behavior of fruit flies. What is the harm in controlling insect behavior, you ask? It is just fruit flies now, but it could take us rapidly down the slippery path to human mind control. I don't care how many safeguards you pile on that invention, it's not something we want in the human toolbox."

George-776: “I was constantly monitoring what Mr. Messenger was doing. There was nothing hazardous at the level at which he was experimenting.

“Mind control, Mr. Homeby, is not inherently dangerous. If you wave a steak in front of a hungry dog, that is mind control: You are controlling what it thinks about. Is that dangerous?

“That is the level to which Mr. Messenger’s techniques had risen. Your reaction was a human-instinct-thinking-based overreaction. It was not based on cost-benefit thinking or risk-reward thinking or with awareness of what defensive technologies were being incorporated into the process and, as a result, has caused a lot more damage than benefit.

“Think about the benefits: What mother, what child, would not want a pill that made doing home work exciting? What person, old or young, would not want New Year’s Resolutions to come true? What person would not want the perseverance to make their heart-felt dreams come true? This is the upside potential of Mr. Messenger’s aspirations.”

Homeby: “What tyrant would not want his subjects to think he was always right? What advertiser would not want his campaigns to always be 110% successful? What cult leader would not want everyone to believe he or she had found the one true way? These are the kinds of abuses mind control tools open up. Time and time again it has been demonstrated that when even primitive mind control clashes with the harsh realities of the world, humanity loses and loses big time. We should not risk that kind of damage enhanced a thousand-fold.”

By the time it is over, I feel I have watched a good debate: I’ve learned a lot, and the right answer is not immediately obvious to me. But it sure does seem like something where a decision is important.

Chapter Twelve

Heads Up From Anton

Dahlia—

Need to talk before next class. There's a class audit coming up.

—Anton

Oh, dear! This sounds too much like an IRS audit. I'm getting nervous already. I call Anton.

"No need to get nervous," he assures me, sounding like a nurse at a dentist's office. "We can talk now, or you can come in ten minutes early for your next class."

"We should talk now," I say decisively.

"OK," he grins, "the borough licenses our school, and they want to be sure all our 'i's are dotted and 't's crossed. Specifically, they want to be sure certain topics are covered in certain ways. I cover 99% of what they ask for with routine paper work, but once in a while…"

"Didn't we just have a school board election? A controversial one?"

Anton winces, "That we did, and it is 'Judge Dredd'… sorry, Ms. Antonelli, who will be attending. But don't worry, all our 'i's are dotted and 't's crossed."

Class Audit

The audit is routine… like a root canal is routine. Sigh!

Ms. Antonelli comes into class announcing, "Please don't change a thing for me," and plops her personal recorder down on the table. The recorder announces, "This class will be monitored for quality control and training purposes. The personal information will be anonymized," and it repeats that message every fifteen minutes. With that kind of entrance, I have to introduce her immediately, and everyone gives her a curt and annoyed welcome.

I try to take her advice and conduct the class as I normally do. I begin with, "For this lesson, we will talk about how much creations should be involved in early child raising. Mankind was using tools to help raise children even in Stone Age times—toys have been found in prehistoric sites. As we have gotten more civilized, the variety of tools used in child raising has grown more elaborate just as all other tool use has.

"And discussions among women about which tools to use have probably dated back to the beginning of language use. So, having discussions about how to use creations is part of a long, long tradition."

"I should say so. I remember my mother and aunt having discussions about how often to give a pacifier," says Janet.

"They date back to at least medieval times," Jaden announces as Mr. Trivia, then backs off a bit by adding, "… so I would guess that conversation dates back a bit, too."

Ms. Antonelli chirps in, "Technology is nice, but the human touch is necessary for wholesome child development. So once an hour, a baby should be picked up and carried around by a human for ten minutes."

I continue, "The arsenal of baby products has been growing exponentially for decades. And, not surprisingly, there are now products to help pick products. This is where creations first began to fit in—they acted as assistant product pickers.

"Few people complained about that use of creations. But when the intelligent rockers started showing up, the murmurs about appropriateness got a lot louder."

Antonelli again, "Babies can pick up vibes from a mother's

activities, so if you want your baby to be literary, you should read good literature while he or she is in your womb."

I continue, "There have been some recent high-profile, if marginal, adaptations of creations to child care. You may recall the case of Annie Z, the anencephaly case—a baby born without the top of her brain—who had a cyber installed. Her parents were rich, kind of nerdy, and hyper-pro-life. She is two years old now, alive, and can walk and talk."

"And there's still a lot of question about how human she is," says Jaden.

"And I've seen the latest video. She is really strange, especially how she talks," adds Jaina.

Antonelli, "Too much sex during pregnancy will make the child promiscuous as a teenager."

Adrian gets back on topic, "She talks like a cyber because she is one… except for her body." He adds matter-of-factly, "I'm not sure why people would expect anything else."

"Because she has a soul," Miranda jumps in.

Adrian has a gleam in his eye like he is ready to jump on that with both feet, but instead thinks better of it and says nothing.

I continue, "As we can see, we may be light years from the Stone Age, but there's still a lot to talk about on what kinds of tools we should use in baby raising."

The first part of the class feels like someone's in-bred Arkansas aunt has crashed a bridge party. Whenever Ms. Antonelli opens her mouth, something completely irrelevant comes out, and when it is advice she justifies it with urban legend. Her recipes for solving the world's problems sound like a delightful pastiche of California Fruitcake garnished with East Coast Flakery.

Well… it would have been delightful if it had been a comedy routine on some vid channel. But she is here in person and as a person of authority—I think she stepped on more toes than we have in the class room. In our work Ben, Janet, Adrian, Ruby, and I have encountered this kind of thing before. We hold our tongues. It is Jaina who breaks.

She raises her hand and asks, "You're an elected official, right?"

"Yes," she responds.

"Just who elected you?"

Ms. Antonelli is just a bit taken aback, "The people of the 12th Brooklyn precinct."

"The nomads? You are in here on the nomad vote?" Jaina snorts.

Antonelli darkens at that, "The 'nomads' as you call them are just as much citizens as everyone else. I appeal to them as much as I did all the other fine citizens of the 12th precinct. Now that *I* have the mandate, there are going to be some changes."

"Oh my," I think, "This doesn't sound like the 'i's and 't's are going to stay dotted and crossed much longer."

Ms. Antonelli turns off the recorder, packs her stuff, and gets ready to leave. Before she does she announces, "Since you all seem so interested, I'll give you my preliminary assessment of this class: While the class seems to have met the previous standards, it will not pass the upcoming standards. The Board of Education is drafting new standards built around the theme of 'A human education for human babies'. This class is not spending enough time on *human* bonding and building *human* karma into our children. This faddish concept that a human child can become a better human if much of its development is handled by cybers is nonsense. If a child is going to grow up human, it must be raised by humans.

"I will see to it that this is emphasized in future curricula."

She looks around… daring…

"Luddite!" shouts Jaina.

There is triumph in Ms. Antonelli's eyes, "That attitude, my dear, will cost you. There's a new wave coming to Brooklyn, and if you keep that attitude it will wash you away!"

Finally it's over. The rest of the class feels like attending a wake for a teetotaling preacher. It's been a rough day. I'm glad it's done. I hope next week we can get back to class business without interruptions.

The Colony Raid

First

Dahlia—

I won't be making class

—Annette
then
Dahlia—
I will be making class after all
—Annette

The "why" for this flip-flop is all over the news: Annette's colony has been raided by the state authorities and they are taking away all the children! There are pictures of dozens of police cars with flashing lights, commandeered school buses being filled with kids, and helicopters flying overhead. What tears your heart out is watching dozens of school age children being lead like the innocents they are into the school buses to be taken who knows where! They are mostly behind blankets to protect their identities, but the blankets are widely enough spaced that the parade of kids is quite visible.

There are distraught women in anachronistic dresses standing outside homes and a school, and grim-faced colony men in jeans and reed hats forming a linked-arm circle around the entrance to the incongruously large and elaborate temple building—I saw it in person when I visited, but in this view it looks like part of a movie set. Facing them are equally grim-faced state troopers with uniforms, dark glasses, and Smokey the Bear hats. There is an occasional, furtive long-shot of snipers backing up the troopers. The troopers and the colony men are negotiating over something. And of course, dozens of media people swirling are around collecting sound bites of people saying the obvious.

It is a stranger than fiction sight, and Annette is here watching it with the rest of us! She is holding back tears. I can't tell if they are of fear, concern, rage, or all of the above.

When the pictures start to repeat what we've already seen, she starts explaining, "We've had our differences with the state Child Protective Services people for a long time. We view them as Nanny Statists, and they feel we recklessly endanger our children. There have been other issues as well."

"I'm betting there's money involved in those other issues," snorts Jaina.

She looks sharply at her; we all do. She retreats a bit and Annette answers, "Yes. We have a lot of plural marriages, and the CPS has never figured out how to deal with that. Neither has the state welfare system. We apply for things, and some of our detractors say we are exploiting loopholes… or outright lying. We say they are lying back to keep us from what's rightfully ours."

"Ouch," I say.

"The townies nearby are the worst. We work hard on our self-sufficiency, and they say we cost them jobs because we won't buy stuff from them. They also say we are hypocrites, and we aren't as self-sufficient as we say we are because we steal stuff.

"It's not true!… Well, not very true. We have a lot of teenagers, and we do train them to solve their own problems. But we also teach them to respect the law!" But her face says Annette is recalling some times when the kids had stepped over the line, even in the colony's eyes.

"What's going on now?" asks Ben.

"Someone phoned in to a child abuse hotline that she was forced to marry when she was thirteen and now her two year old child is being abused. CPS says that all the children in the colony are at risk, so they all have to be moved out."

"What! All this based on one phone call?" I say.

Annette nods. "And they haven't found the caller. They are keeping the name anonymous, but the word is out that they are still looking, and they haven't found her.

"They won't find her, either! We don't marry thirteen-year-olds! We marry fifteen-year-olds with judicial consent." She looks around sharply.

"… Different strokes," says Ruby. Annette looks relieved at that.

"What happens now?" I ask.

"I… I… I don't know. That's why I came to class. I talked with the people there, and we agreed that my being there wasn't going to make any difference. It would just add to confusion and congestion. And… it might help to have someone meet people in New York, so I should stay. For me, for now, it's business as usual."

She looks grim, and we all share her deep, deep worry. What can she do? What can we do?

"You have our full support in this, Annette. I'm saying that for all of us," I say. I don't have to look around for approval.

< < < * > > >

By the next week, this had turned from SNAFU to FUBAR for the CPS, as some of my military friends would put it. The tipster turned out to be a fraudster, and while the moral grounds for the raid remained strong in some eyes, the legal grounds turned to quicksand.

We in New York were all busy contacting people. Back at the colony, the state was discovering that the logistics of finding new foster homes for four hundred children at the same time was proving daunting. The colony lawyers were gathering evidence for a counter-suit of child abuse being conducted by the CPS for their negligent handling of the children.

And there was precedent—this was not the first time a state's protective services had raided a polygamist colony, and in the more recent cases—which were over fifty years ago—the state had had to turn tail and run from what turned into a big blunder. Things were looking up.

Annette was looking more comfortable when she came to the next class, but she was still looking grim, "No matter how this turns out, we will remember."

She then got very gracious and thanked everyone sincerely for their help. Things were certainly looking a lot less scary than they were last week.

The "Nomad Spring" Blossoms

For the next few weeks, it does seem as if Ms. Antonelli is on the leading edge of some wave. There are announcements of shakeups at the board of education, and those are followed by announcements of changes in our curriculum guidelines. Anton is not pleased, and neither am I, but what can we do?

And there are teeth in those pronouncements: We are hearing about classes at other schools getting decertified. Anton, God bless him, seems to be keeping Child Champs ahead of the storm, but that means lots of inconvenience for us teachers. The guidelines of what we have to cover are getting a whole lot more picayunish.

And it is not just Brooklyn. Last year, there had been a scandal when the town manager of a new resort town in North Dakota had tried to improve his town's image by booting out nomads. The project was insane from day one: How in the world could anyone develop an upscale resort in North Dakota? What were nomads doing in North Dakota? The situation got real ugly and high-profile when the Nomad supporters dug up that the mayor was both a convicted sociopath and had been raised exclusively by cyber parents.

Of course, the background facts behind those lurid headlines were a lot more mundane—the sociopath conviction was for a sexting incident when the mayor was in middle school, and the "nomads" were nomad wannabes, high schoolers from a nearby community that existed to maintain a national park. But that hadn't stopped a wave of outrage from sweeping through nomad communities all over the US. The outrage had started as protesting and then turned political, and Ms. Antonelli was part of that wave.

In fact, the real tragedy of that incident wasn't the nomads, but the fate of Charles McDougal, the town manager. Twenty years ago, McDougal had been a child prodigy. He had made headlines briefly as the first child raised by two cyber parents and for winning a science fair when he was eight years old. But fate had not been kind—maybe there is karma. First the sexting business, then last year, he had taken the position of town manager of this resort that was just as ill-starred as his career was.

Legend has it that the Wounded Knee Resort was started on a bet made by Harold Koch, a Koch family heir. He boasted he could develop a first-tier resort community anywhere in the US. His drinking buddy of the time put up a US map and handed him a dart. Koch was aiming for Mount Rushmore, and he was a decent dartsman, but his buddy jerked the map after he let fly. They both had a good laugh at that, and that should have been the end of it, but that buddy held him to his bet.

Until last year, Wounded Knee had been called Fort Beaufort, and it had been an obscure money hole. But Koch was determined, and McDougal was brought in to shake things up. He started with some profile-raising. He changed the name to Wounded Knee, even though that historic site is across the state line in South Dakota and close to Nebraska not North Dakota. He stepped on other toes in his profile-raising and finally tromped on a big one with this bums rushing nomads incident. He resigned, with criminal charges threatened, but by then the protest wave had developed a life of its own. The Nomad Spring had begun.

Jaina hadn't been far off the mark in calling Antonelli a Luddite, but that didn't help the situation any, and Child Champs suffered for it—we were now on Ms. Antonelli's radar, and she was a sign of the times.

Chapter Thirteen

The Game Changes

As it turns out, things do not get better, and the Antonelli storm does not blow over. It rages.

Before my next-to-last class with this group, Anton calls a staff meeting. Whatever is coming, it won't be good.

He calls the meeting to order and announces, "Folks, these are trying times.

"I've been trying to accommodate Ms. Antonelli and the board, but… in a word… I can't." He sighs.

"The changes I've passed on to you are just a beginning for the board. Sadly, they mark the end for Child Champs in Brooklyn. Following this class cycle, I will be shutting down this office in Brooklyn and transitioning Child Champs to virtual… for now. I will be looking for some place I can reestablish a teaching facility in a more technologically tolerant environment.

"Are there any questions?"

On one hand, it is not too big a surprise… but then it is a big surprise! Personally, I was sure Anton was going to be able to rise above this. He'd risen to all other challenges for the last ten years, hadn't he?

Nancy, one of the other teachers, raises her hand, "Online? That's going to kill the image, isn't it?"

"Indeed," he chuckles a bit over the irony, "it presents a marketing challenge.

"But there is something else that has influenced my decision, as well. There is an opportunity coming, a completely different opportunity, and it's a game changer. It's big. It's exciting. And I want to present it to you and your students with a bit of flourish.

"So what I will do is meet with each of your classes personally to discuss this new opportunity. Please let them know that the last class will be a special session."

All of us leave the meeting wondering what is coming up.

The Opt-Out Colony

After Jaden tells us about the Santa Claus suit settlement, we don't see him for two class sessions. We all wonder what's up.

The third session he gives us a call. He is in the Poconos in the Good To Mother Nature Commune, an opt-out commune.

"Come on over for a tour some time," he invites us over the audio-only channel, "These people have their act totally together."

We look around at each other. This is sure crazy-sounding.

"We're happy to hear you're OK, and having a good time," says Ben.

"It's more than a good time. It's enlightening and fulfilling. You really should come visit," he says. He sounds a bit distracted.

"We'll give it some thought here," Ben answers back diplomatically. "Let us have your number, and we'll get back in touch."

"Well, you can't reach me directly, but here's the commune number..." He gives it to us as our eyes widen. No direct phone number? What sort of life is this?

The fourth week he is back, looking thinner and gaunt.

"You're back!" Jaina says as she bounces in the door.

Jaden nods, but doesn't say much more until everyone has come in. Even then he starts slowly.

He opens with, "... It's been quite an experience."

"I can imagine," says Ben.

Jaden looks at him. "Not likely.

"I've been indoctrinated for four weeks now. I was hoping for a harmonious paradise on Earth. I was promised that! But it's been a hell instead.

"The people I talked to in the City said this place was a place where humans could be humans. That part sounded real good. I was tired of getting fucked around.

"The problem was these people had only one definition of how to be human. 'There is a right way, a wrong way, and the Good To Mother Nature way,' I was told in an indoctrination session about a week after I arrived. At the time I didn't believe what I was hearing, but it turned out to be true… so true."

"What happened?" asks Jaina.

"Well, being a newbie, I was assigned the shit detail, literally. I got to move the 'night soil', they called it, from the bed chamber pots and outhouses to the compost piles."

"What's an outhouse?"

Jaden gulps a bit, "Look it up."

Jaina does. "Oh!" and she gulps a bit, too.

"You were that back to Mother Nature, eh?" says Ben.

"Yeah. It was disgusting. And we didn't have to be doing that! We were living in an abandoned resort. They had actually pulled toilets out of the rooms. There were lots of empty rooms but we newbs were bunked six to a room in the old servants quarters.

"But I would have put up with it if I thought I would get some reward for doing so…. Some spiritual reward, that is. I'm not after material reward!"

"Who is?" says Adrian rhetorically.

Jaden looks sharply at Adrian. At first he doesn't like hearing that, but he thinks a bit more, then goes on, "What grated me more and more was this attitude that this was not about just being a non-creation-using place, it was about 'there is only one right way', and that way was decided by the commune leader, a guy named Mr. Harmony. Those people around him worshipped him! What he said went, just because he said it. Those guys around him made sure of that. The rest of the people there just lived with that.

"A couple of days ago, I got fed up and started arguing about some of the choices. For instance, I found out that while we plebs had to live with outhouses, Mr. Harmony and the top boys had kept their running water toilets. When I mentioned that, I was told in no uncertain terms to get with the program or get out. By then they had really pissed me off. I chose to get out… and here I am."

"Sounds like you brushed into a for-real closed cult," says Ben. "Those places can get quite spooky. I'm glad you found that out quickly."

"… Yeah. I found out I didn't like that one…. But I wonder if there's one around I can like? I… I… don't think I can go back to teaching. Those people fucked me over too badly, too."

"You're certainly at a difficult point in life. Have you tried some counseling?" asks Ben.

Jaden laughs, "I don't lack for advice! I get much more than I want all the time now. That's partly why I tried the commune."

"Good point," says Ben and he thinks some more, "Well… if this was fifty years ago, I'd advise what you needed right now was a good woman." He laughs and we all join him. "These days, I guess you'll have to get by with a good creation.

"Let me give this some more thought, Jaden, and see if we can get you on a more successful path. Promise me you'll take at least a week before you join another commune."

Jaden grins, "I can do that. That won't be hard to keep."

With that, we begin the class.

As class ends I remind everyone, "Don't forget that next class is the last one, and it's going to be special. Anton Noidtal, the director, will be giving us a special presentation."

"On what?" asks Ruby.

"On an opportunity coming to us that's beyond just baby making and baby raising. I'll let him give you the details next week. I understand it's really something special."

Andy's Borneo Trip

D—

Headed back. Lunch Thursday next week?

—A

A—

Looking forward to it!

—D

Andy is coming out. What a relief! Sure he had all the modern protections. Well, all you can get in a place that doesn't have avatars. Sheesh! How much can that be? I am so relieved and so looking forward to seeing him again.

He's been blogging about his adventure, but as his adventure has deepened, his communications have gotten sketchier and sketchier—part was bandwidth issues and part was the nature of his adventure, talking too much is either violating company policy or dangerous.

We have lunch at Salucci's again, and boy! he seems to be relishing it. As he comes in, he is constantly looking around and just plain enjoying.

"Good to be home, eh?"

"Oh my, is it!"

We order and he talks.

"We made the final leg of the journey on amphibians. We flew in to an eco-observation refuge thirty kilometers away on a jungle cargo plane. That was quite a thrill in and of itself. This plane was STOL—short take off and landing—and that dirt runway was really short! I looked at the prop after we landed and I didn't say anything, but I swear I saw fresh sap on it! Umm...

"We freshened up and organized at the refuge for a day, then hopped into quietized amphibians. Those were a sight! They were legged. They would swim through the swamps and muck, then walk over what was too solid to swim through.

"This place we were headed was not easy to get to. That's why it is still relatively pristine. But... boy! Not easy to get to is right! God! Miles and miles of muck! Complete with hot and cold running crocs and snakes and dragonflies so big you'd swear they could take off a finger if they had a mind to!

"We wanted to be low profile. The goal of this was to make

friends and build trust. Not that these people haven't seen planes and helicopters by now. But this was at the heart of an area where the regional authorities are working on regrowing the biodiversity. That's why we were there, too. This group I'm working for wanted to check, once again, if there was anything genetically useful in this chunk of jungle.

"Again?"

"Oh yeah. I did some research. This idea that the jungle is chock-full of mysterious and wonderful cures gets strong enough for people to put money behind it every couple of decades. Some young hotshot at a drug company announces they are spending bucks to send out collectors. Some other companies get wind and their young hotshots "me too", then documentarians follow them around for a while and get their rocks off when a collector gets the hot idea to consult a local shaman. One or two things are found, but not enough to warrant the expense, and the idea gets quietly dropped. This time is no different, except expedition costs are cheaper, and we have updated analytical tools to use, and genes are now a lot cheaper to work with than seeds used to be, so... maybe this time."

"Any luck?"

He grins, "You get the decades-old answer: 'We won't know for a while.'"

"But we did go through all the steps: We made friends with the locals—your T-Shirts were a fabulous hit, by the way, thanks again—then did some preliminary searching, then shaman consulting with a documentarian watching, then some more searching. It went smoothly.

"And, my part went well enough that my contractors asked if I was interested in doing more work for them if this project continues. They are looking for a company-mayor liaison."

"Nice!"

It sounds good, but Andy doesn't look happy.

"What's up?" I ask.

"Well... like I said, this has been done before. This is one of the remotest places left on the planet... and we're doing a rerun." He sighs.

"If anything comes of our find, and the project gets a greenlight, they'll have avatar towers installed down there in six months, and the place will be effectively as far away as Long Beach is from Hollywood."

He looks at me, "I want to be doing something new. Not reboots of Jungle Jim episodes."

My heart goes out to him. This is why I love him so and why I broke up with him. He wants to be on the edge, and not in some silly adrenaline-rush sense. He wants to be on the edge in helping humanity. He wants to be an Einstein or an Edison, but creations are covering both of those niches pretty well these days.

"What will you do next?" I ask.

"I'm not sure. This job is done, no matter what the results of our searching.

"I suppose I could apply for that company-mayor liaison if they decide to invest there. If they do, some kind of town will spring up there, and someone will have to keep the peace. Could be interesting in a Wild West sort of way... if there's a greenlight... but that's still a rerun, and these days there's a whole lot of regulations to follow in developing indigenous places. With all that recipe-following, it'll be more like being a chef than a sheriff." He sighs again.

We finish lunch without much more of interest said, but I enjoy it anyway. And then I think, "Oh my! Andy has a special place in my mind again! LOL!"

Maybe I should be checking if I have some pills leftover... and maybe not.

Chapter Fourteen

Anton's Big Picture

Dahlia—

We should talk about last class presentation. Visit my summer home? Next Saturday?

—Anton

Anton's summer home is on the south coast of Martha's Vineyard. There is a drive, but it's not nearly as rigorous as getting to Annette Bushkov's compound. If you want to indulge in nostalgia, you can take a ferry from the Falmouth on the Massachusetts coast to Edgartown. I choose not to, and I land at the airport instead.

Many residents here love boating. They get in real boats and sail them thither and yon. About half are real sailboats, too—the wind powers them.

The front of Anton's house looks old and weathered. When Anton greets me at the door he explains, "This side of the house dates from two hundred years ago. It's a beast to keep up, but I love the look." As we walk in, we pass Anton's "brag wall"—there is some impressive stuff on it: awards, degrees, honorary degrees, and autographed photos.

When we get inside, things are quite contemporary. The view south is stunning. This is called a beach house, but it isn't really on the beach. It is on a bluff over an inlet, and the ocean is a quarter mile away, crashing up on the real beach which spreads entirely across the inlet there. What surrounds the house is wind-swept dune grass, with a circle of strategically planted bushes and oak trees which act as a windbreak for the house itself.

We sit at a table in the living room that takes full advantage of the view. In spite of myself, I am starting to feel relaxed and inspired.

"Dahlia, you and the class have been on quite an odyssey, I suspect."

I nod.

"Let me give you some more perspective before I make my proposition to you.

"As you look around now, and reflect on what you've seen over the past few months, does humanity look threatened to you?"

"… No?"

"It is," Anton says grimly. "It doesn't look like it, but it is.

"What is threatening humanity is its success. We have conquered adversity. We have conquered natural calamity. We have conquered resource depletion. We have even conquered age.

"And therein lies the problem: Mankind is an evolved creature. For thousands… no… millions of generations, he has evolved to conquer adversity, as all life forms on earth have.

"The problem… the huge problem… is… we've won!

"… So… what do we do for encore?"

"Enjoy the fruits of our success?" I offer.

"That is retiring," Anton grins, "and mankind did not evolve to retire."

"And there is some more urgency to this problem, as well. Mankind has already evolved his successor species—the creations."

"Creations? Our helpers?… Some people have always worried that they would rebel and take over earth, but there are plenty of safeguards… aren't there?"

Anton smiles. "It's not a question of nefarious plot. The threat is much more of a… whimper… than that.

"The creations are well-designed to live in the world as we experience it today. We now live in a known world. We understand it. Science has removed the mysteries. We can still have surprises, of course, but nothing is going to happen on earth that creations can't understand and handle.

"Mankind, on the other hand, evolved to handle a world full of mystery. We are well-adapted to handling the unknown, while creations are well-adapted to handling the known. Earth is now a well-known place.

"So, if mankind is now living in retirement, what's next for mankind?" He waits patiently for me to answer.

"... Death?" I say, not liking what I am saying.

He grins, "Death... *or moving on*! Moving to places where the world a person lives in is still an exciting mystery and full of unknowns. There mankind will thrive again, and do what he's best at doing.

"Mankind's 'fit', mankind's destiny, is to confront huge mysteries and solve them enough to live and thrive. That's what mankind does best, and in that environment creations can comfortably play their role as helpful tools. In that environment mankind and creations are symbiotes. In earth's environment today, creations are a successor species waiting for mankind to realize he has outlived his usefulness.

"That's why this Mars colonizing program is so important: It's a key step in mankind's survival. Mankind must adapt to Mars, adapt to other places in the Solar System, and adapt to traveling to the stars. This *must* be mankind's destiny. That or... retiring... and letting his successor species, the creations, eulogize his passing."

"I... I... I never thought of things that way," I say.

"Few people have. It's not a comfortable thought, and these are comfortable times we live in."

"What can I do?"

"Fully back the Mars program. We must get mankind self-sufficiently settled around the Solar System, and we must get him headed to the stars."

"That doesn't sound so hard."

"Your time, your enthusiasm, and your DNA will all help." he said confidently.

Anton looks happy. He's made a convert.

But it isn't enough! Anton has worked this hard and just converted me. Just me! This is a human race problem, and it can't be handled as just another human hobby idea! There are billions of those, and most are a lot more comfortable to think about.

This would take some more thought, some careful thought.

"In the meantime, would you like a tour of my humble abode?"

We walk around a bit, then go down to the dock and get into a sailboat—a real sailboat! It's a small one. He launches us, and we sail to the beach. This ride is fully as wild as Annette's colony road ride. Those sail boats really do lean way, way over! The good news is that as I keep climbing to the high side in stark terror, Anton says, "You're doing it right!" and laughs heartily like an old sea captain.

At the beach it is windy and cool, but I do take some time to build a sand castle. I've loved doing that since I discovered the sandbox in our kindergarten playground.

We talk and think, and talk and think. I don't say so, but I am thinking, "It still isn't enough!"

Anton talks about how mankind is a boom species. That's why we have the Neolithic Parks. The creations are openly enthusiastic about wanting to dismantle those because they are the source of so much human suffering, and they aren't alone. There are periodic publicity campaigns and lawsuits. The lawsuits are to dismantle the parks and toss someone in jail for condoning the torture and child abuse that occurs in them.

"But if those are closed down, it is certain death for the human species at the next world-wide calamity," he says grimly.

The ride back feels entirely different and a lot more relaxing. Anton says that is because the wind is at our back now.

At the end of the day I head home. It was short, but it has been a fascinating trip in so many ways.

Jaden and Janet

At small talk before the next class, Jaden and Janet have a happy announcement... somewhat happy, anyway.

Janet says, "Jaden and I were able to get an appeal launched to his conviction. We got his trial declared a mistrial, and his status is now back to that of accused, not convicted. The ACLU is taking an interest in this, so it's not likely to be a railroading the next time it goes to court."

I look around and spoke for all of us when I say, "Thank you, Janet. And… Wow! What a lucky guy you are, Jaden, to have her for a friend!" We all applaud.

Janet holds up her hand, "We don't have a happy ending, yet, folks. But we've got a second try, and there should be a lot fewer cheap shots this time."

But she is just not counting chickens before they hatch. It is clearly real good news.

"What about LAU-TV channel? This would seem a perfect fit for that?" asks Ruby.

"I thought about that, Ruby, but decided against it. Yeah, we have a wronged man and a bureaucracy grinding him up and spitting him out. That would get ratings, for sure. But the bureaucracy grinding him up and spitting him out is a union. That aspect would strike terror in the hearts of most LAU-TV producers. It would add a lot of uncertainty which means delays. The people who would take the most interest in this as a polemic would be Libertarians. That market would be a pretty small sideshow."

"I see your point," says Ruby.

As class is about to begin I see Anton out in the hall. My heart starts to beat faster with sudden anticipation. This should be good. I hurry to introduce him.

The Last Class

And so the last class—the special one—begins. I start by introducing Anton, "Today we have a special guest speaker: Anton Noidtal, director and owner of Child Champs," I announce.

We all greet him, and he begins.

"I'm here to talk to you about a program the Space Agency is sponsoring, and it's one some of you may be interested in. It's one that I certainly am.

"The Space Agency is supporting setting up a colony on Mars. Not a resort, not a science station, not a factory, but a large population colony where humans will live permanently and which they will come to call their home, and so will their grandchildren.

In a few years it will become self-sustaining, and be another step in man's settling the whole solar system, and beyond that, the stars.

"… Why should we be interested?" asks Ben.

"Because it's a place where you can be human again. It's a place where your human ingenuity will matter. It's a place where you can make a difference, not be just another cog in an increasingly well-ordered world—a world which has become better and better suited to cybers and creations. It's a place where there will be surprises—something human people in biological bodies are still the best-designed creatures in the universe to deal with… well, the universe we know about anyway."

Janet asks, "Have we come that far? What about the risks? How will we get fed the right food? How will old people like Ben and me get our medical care?"

Anton laughs a bit, "This is not a digger cult. We can do digger just fine here on Earth. The bots will come too. Much of our food is nanobot-made now, and that is just as easy to do on Mars as it is here. The same for medicine. We can make it there as easily as we can here.

"In fact, we've had the technology to colonize for two decades. What has held this project back is worries about risk. That very human emotion to save the children has had some surprise consequences." He grins as he says, "One of those has been to 'save' Mars from colonizing humans.

"This is not to say there are not risks. There are. Accidents will happen. Surprises will happen. People will die and people will be amazed.

"But humans are designed to be mortal. Up until twenty years ago, there were no immortals. Humans are also designed to take risks." He looks around a bit before he continues, "This is not a popular point of view these days, but I feel our current trends towards cutting off risk-taking in the name of saving the children have gone way overboard. They are badly twisting our social thinking."

"Isn't that just adapting our thinking to the environment we live in now?" asks Jaden.

Anton smiles, "You bring up a good point, Jaden. Our environment today is certainly not the Stone Age environment our brains and bodies are best adapted for.

"But that's the point! What we are living in now, here on Earth, is not what humans are well-adapted for. It's too secure. It's too predictable. We are best adapted for a world full of mysteries and unknowns. These days we are going to find that environment on Mars and beyond. This is where humans should be now... at least some of us."

"There is one more point you should know about. I said biological bodies—not human bodies—for a reason. On the Mars colony, we will have enough technology to transfer intelligences between cyber and biological. And we will use that technology there. You can use your Earth body when you want to, but your intelligence won't be restricted to it."

We look around at each other. I say, "I've heard speculations on such. But isn't that unethical and illegal?"

"It is here on Earth, but Mars is not Earth," he grins again. "With time, there will be quite a few things OK there that are too scary, technically, for Earth society to accept."

He looks around the classroom, looks each of us in the face, "You are all here because you want to take part in a great adventure: the great adventure of raising a child. What I'm asking you now is do you want to take part in an even greater adventure: that of settling a new world? Carving a new world from a new wilderness? I'm asking you as a group because a group you have become. For weeks now you've been sharing your triumphs and disappointments, and you've had both. You are becoming tight.

"I'm giving each of you the site which describes this new colonizing program and the details of what it takes to qualify and what you can expect there. Take a moment to go through that and see if you have any questions."

Anton waits patiently while the class goes cross-eyed for a bit and absorbs this new information. Miranda touches the face of her hand-held phone every now and then.

"You're a founding member of the Mars Colonizing Steering Committee? Wow!" says Jaina. Then with a cross between admiration and suspicion, "Are you like some kind of high mucky-muck government official then?"

Anton smiles at her, "This has been a long-time dream for me, Jaina. To make it happen, I had to engage the people and creations who had the right resources to make it happen. So, yes,

I'm now some kind of high mucky-muck *NGO* official. I leave the government work for others." He laughs.

Adrian speaks up, "I know the creation establishment has resisted this for a long time. Have they changed their minds?"

"They now recognize that colonies throughout the solar system can be traded off against closing the Neolithic Parks on Earth. As much as they dislike putting people into danger in space, if they can take people out of danger on Earth, they will give it their support."

"Will they accept people with... diverse beliefs?" asks Annette.

"Colonies have a long history of accepting people with diverse beliefs. The creations recognize that, and this one will be no exception. One of my contributions as a steering committee member is making sure the colony project is structured to be diverse. Diversity and redundancy will add to security and survivability. This will be an adventure, an experience full of surprises. We can't know now which policies will work best, so trying many makes a lot of sense.

"And your group, Annette, with its long habit of living close to the land and being resourceful in dealing with surprises, should make it comparatively comfortable in adapting to this new environment."

Annette smiles back at Anton.

Anton looks at Rubyzin, "Ruby, what are your thoughts?"

Ruby doesn't hesitate, "Oh, I'm an entertainer. The world is my oyster." She laughs. "I guess more than the world these days. I've been offered gigs on the moon and Mars."

"Are you saying this is irrelevant to you?"

"Yes. I travel all the time. What difference does this make?"

"Will your child travel with you?"

Ruby looks a little surprised and thinks a moment before she says, "... Good point."

Anton leaves her to muse on that. He turns to Jaina. "What are your thoughts, Jaina?"

"It sounds like super fun... for a while. But I'm still an Earth girl. I've got lots of friends here."

"Are they the face-to-face type?"

"Some of them are... a few... well, a couple. Most are on the net, now that you mention it."

"Dahlia tells me you're interested in raising Mars babies. Why not do that where they are native?"

She thinks about it and brightens, "I could be a lot more effective there, couldn't I. I wouldn't have to constantly be saying, 'When you get to where you'll live, things will be... whatever.' Yeah, that would be good. It's not like I can't come back to Earth for vacations."

"So true," assures Anton, "and year by year it's getting faster and cheaper. The constant acceleration propulsion technology is coming of age now."

He turns to Miranda, "You've traveled a long way to get here. What do you think about traveling a bit further?"

She frowns, "I have my family to think of. My mother is very old."

Anton brightens at that, "The colony settlements will have the most up-to-date medical facilities. You and all your family should find it a lot easier to get patched up there than here. Once you're there, there should be a lot less red tape and hoop-jumping."

Miranda likes the sound of that.

He turns to Adrian. "I don't want to sound like a PR hack, but you're one of the more resourceful people here: You've grown a thriving business."

He doesn't laugh it off. He is thinking hard. "I'm glad you recognize it's no walk in the park.... I'm wondering if I'm too specialized? Business is what I know best.... That and gene editing."

"Any new colony is going to have a lot of business dealings. They won't be the same kind or in the same environment, but they will be all about exploiting opportunities and dealing with people, creations, and Mother Nature to make them happen."

Now Adrian smiles, "That sounds familiar."

He comes back to Jaden again. He just looks and waits.

Jaden finally speaks, "I'm a union man.... Or, at least I have been one. I admit that these last few weeks have been quite a test of my union spirit. Will collectivism have any meaning, any importance, in a Mars colony? Are there going to be evil bosses I can rail against. Are there going to be dark conspiracies that I and my fellow workers have to protect ourselves from?"

Anton doesn't say a thing. He just waits.

Jaden continues, "I… I… I guess if those are irrelevant that's a good thing." He looks up, "There will still be dangers, though, won't there? Of course!… Which means I can keep an eye out for the safety of others." He brightens at that thought. "Yeah, my ideals can still have meaning. We all still need to be sure we are as safe as we can be… and still get things done, of course. Yeah, I'm in."

And finally he looks at me.

I say, "I got into this to raise babies, not wear a coonskin cap. But you make a good point. There certainly seem to be a lot of 'Yes, buts…' involved in baby-raising these days. I teach this class, but sometimes I'm real disappointed in what I have to teach. I want to raise a baby the way I think is right, not the way everybody in the neighborhood thinks is right. Do you think that's going to be possible on Mars?"

"I think it's not only possible, I think it will be mandatory. Mars is eight-to-twenty four minutes from Earth on the fastest communication link. How is some Earth bureaucrat or monitoring creation going to look over your shoulder real time?

"Not that some won't try at first, but you can simply tell them 'Get real!'… What are they going to do?"

"… Live with it." I say with a grim grin.

"Just as you will have to," he cautions. "I'm sure there will be a few times when you'll dearly wish that big, expert help was a lot closer. But those will be rare compared to the most-of-the-times when you're satisfied that you're doing the right thing. And doing a real good job with the resources at hand. And you will be," he grins. "You've been training for this a long time."

He looks around at all of us, "Pardon me if I sound a little megalomaniacal but… you've all been training for this. You haven't been aware of it, but this is what you've been living for. You're all human, and humans live for solving the mysterious. These days, we will find the mysterious on Mars.

"Are there any more questions?"

There are none. He's given us a lot to think about.

"I'll let you get back to your studies. Thank you."

He walks out, and we all think for about a half minute before I say, "OK. Mars project or not, that pretty well wraps up this course. Let's review, answer last questions, then it's party time!"

BOOK THREE:

THE NEW BEGINNING

Chapter Fifteen

After Class

Going to Mars... and living there!

Anton had proposed it. Now we all have to think about it.

It's pretty heady stuff! Move to Mars. Not just pull up stakes on the Big Apple, but pull up stakes on the whole planet Earth as well!

It's crazy!... But he has made some compelling arguments. I can sure feel what he was talking about.

We schedule with each other, and the class gets together for our first post-class gathering. We reserve a room at Salucci's.

After some small talk I open the main event.

"Who's been thinking about Anton's Mars proposal?"

At first there is silence, and for a scary moment I fear I've told a bad joke, but Ben responds.

"It's crazy!... But Janet and I have been giving it a lot of thought.

"We've been thinking about what we humans are doing here on Earth. Our class encounter with Ms. Antonelli sure brought home that times are changing here in America, too.

"But those know-nothing nomads are just the icon. They indicate that humans on earth are steadily transforming into soap opera entertainment for the creations." He shakes his head. It is not a comfortable thought.

"You're saying she's important? That's nuts!" affirms Jaina in her own special way.

"She's not the only one," Ben continues. "There have been other similar changes going on around the world. You know those geishas that Dahlia showed us that video about?" We nod. "Well, I was just reading that the East Africans have come up with another use for that concept. Some entrepreneur there is launching a project to grow albinos, with plans for harvesting them for their magic mojo."

"I thought you said those people there were getting more civilized?" says Jaina after we all think about that a moment.

"They are. But they are getting more prosperous as well, which means they can afford to support more of their expensive local customs. For them, this is much like cultivating rhinoceros for the horn—something the East Asians still dearly adore. And for something more local, it's like cultivating foxes and raccoons, and hunting hounds and horses.

There is silent thinking on that until Ruby changes the subject by bursting out, "But Mars! There's nothing there! No culture, anyway."

"That's what makes it so exciting," says Adrian. "You're starting from scratch there."

"Well, not quite from scratch," Janet adds. "This is a Space Agency-sponsored colonizing program. Through the Space Agency the various earth national governments have spent billions to set up infrastructure there already."

"Mere billions. Pfft!" scoffs Adrian. "Mars is a white canvas with a single black dot on it."

"Is it true about the good medical?" asks Miranda.

"It should be," I say. "Jaina and I visited one of the Mars baby labs, and they were sparing no expense there." Jaina nods.

"Compared to the cost of providing basic life support, the cost of adding state-of-the-art medical will be small. And this isn't some kind of slave colony. The Space Agency needs to attract people. It should be good," adds Janet.

"What will people do there?" asks Jaden.

"Making it suitable for even more people will be task number one for a long time," answers Adrian. "Much of that will be basic infrastructure building, but the creations will handle most of that.

The interesting part for people will be dealing with the surprises. I guarantee you that some things we do there will be easier than we expected, some things will be harder, and there will be a whole bunch of things where people say, 'Eh? You're doing what?'… surprise things! Those will be the most fun, too, and probably the most valuable.

"As the folks already on Mars say, 'Mars isn't Earth.'"

"You mean like UV-process harvesting?" says Jaden.

"Exactly! Who would have figured it was cheaper to lay out some kinds of stuff on Mars' surface for solar UV to cold-roast than to build sun lamps and shine them on stuff sitting in freezers here on Earth? It's a surprise, and it's now a thriving industry on Mars. And humans discovered that."

"Sort of like your fruit flies?" I add.

He winces a little at the memory, but his answer is enthusiastic, "Yeah! The humans on Mars had to do a lot of trial-and-error to figure out that UV technique. They did it, and now they, and we, are getting the payoff."

Annette is connected by conference call. She muses, "This looks like a place where our lifestyle could be appreciated. We've long worked on doing things with as little creation inter… involvement as possible."

Janet frowns, "The match on that might not be as good as you think, Annette. The people on Mars don't shun creation help. They take all they can get. It's just that there's a lot creations can't do there."

Annette nods, "Point taken. I brought up this project with the colony leaders when I returned, and there has been some interest. But I will be sure to point out what you've said.… Still if the creations are *helping* humans… and *needed* to do so… this could be compatible with our colony philosophy. It's worthy of more discussion around here."

What follows is silence. After a minute I ask cautiously, "Well… does anyone think this project is completely nuts?"

No one speaks up. No one raises their hand.

I get bold, "Should we plan on forming a Mars Colony Club and go through the information/application process?"

To my amazement, there are nods all around! Everyone there

is willing to take the first step toward pulling up stakes and starting a new life on a strange world!

It feels very strange, but very good!

"OK. I'll start the paperwork rolling. One thing I know we'll all have to do is take the MAT—Mars Application Test. I'll set up a schedule for some class prep for that. Whew! The training never ends."

I laugh, and we all do.

The Mars Colony Club

I have my bot jump through the hoops to formally start a club and apply for it to get into the Mars program. The Big Apple Mars Colony Club name is taken, not surprisingly, so I call ours the Child Champs Mars Colony Club.

My bot receives and passes around the list of what it is going to take to qualify. The list of requirements, as summarized by my bot, is surprisingly simple:

Pass a general competence test: Meaning, have a college degree or expertise in something technical that creations on Mars can't handle well.

Pass a means test: This is a proxy for demonstrating that you really have handled problem-solving in the real world well.

Pass the MAT, the Mars Aptitude Test: This is to demonstrate you can still learn and have learned some Mars basics.

Pass the MST, the Mars Simulation Test: This is the Mars environment version of a Neolithic Park sim and is conducted here on Earth. This is to demonstrate you do have a clue about what you're getting into and still think it's a good idea.

Pass all of the above and you get a slot on the queue for a ship berth, and you get to start planning seriously about what you're taking along and what you're leaving behind.

< < < * > > >

At our second class meeting, and first formal club meeting, we have two surprise guests: Andy and George-776! They both want to join the club.

Andy tells us, "I made inquiries with the Mars Colony Program people and got word this club was forming. Mind if I join?"

I have no problem with that.

George-776 tells us, "You humans aren't the only ones that are dissatisfied with how things are changing here on earth. My experience with the Fruit Fly Raid was not an isolated incident. There are controversies that rage through the creation community that humans don't hear about. The Fruit Fly Raid happened because what Mr. Homeby was complaining about resonated with a point of contention within the creation community, and I ended up on the sharp, pointed, receiving end of that point of contention.

"I was outraged, and the issue has not been resolved to my satisfaction. Something like it could happen again, so I am... how do some of you humans put it... out of here!... And with your club, if you're willing to have me."

I vouch for Andy and Adrian vouches for George-776. We have a quick vote and both are admitted.

< < < * > > >

We talk about the requirements. They looked straightforward enough.

Janet points out, "This program is new. This means it can change. I would recommend we move as quickly as we can. In particular, I'm looking at the means test. I can see that becoming a target for lots of groups demanding equality. It could change in some fashion, and change quickly. And the change won't be good for us."

"Why not?" asks Jaden.

"The change is likely to be from a means test to a tax—have the emigrants help pay their way—and from that into a subsidy for those who can't pay the tax—make it fair for everyone."

"What's wrong with that?"

Janet looks at Jaden carefully, "Mars isn't Earth. If a person is having trouble being productive on Earth, and they can't change that when they get to Mars, they become a liability, not an asset. Mars Colony doesn't need extra liability in this stage of its development."

"You're presuming that—"

"Let's save philosophy for the ship ride, folks," I interrupt. "While we're still on Earth, let's concentrate on getting us off-planet. Who is ready to take the MAT? Who needs some help?"

Jaden and Janet back off, and Jaina raises her hand, "MAT and PAT. I want to do better on that PAT, and this time I'm ready to let my cybertutor help me. I still think I want to be raising babies when I'm on Mars."

Adrian says, "I should be ready next week. What kind of schedule do we want to set up?"

The rest of the meeting devotes itself to hashing out a schedule for prepping and testing that all members of the club can stick with, and presuming that goes well, what date we want for a berth.

Passing the MST

I'm on the surface of Mars, as in, above ground! And it's cold! Bone-chilling cold!

And that's not a euphemism!

It's that way because my suit power supply has failed! It happened in mid-bounce and I've now rolled to a stop facing the black, star-filled sky. What do I do now?

I reach down to my chest—a lot of effort without power—and manually move the power plug from the main fuel cell to the emergency. My suit comes to life! My gosh, I'm so relieved!

I check my revived head-up display, click over to the Mayday Channel, and in half a second announce, "Mayday Control. Have experienced severe suit malfunction. I'm headed directly for rescue center Charlie-One-Four."

"Roger Man-Eater-Four. Have received your suit diagnostic. Will send a recovery cart in ten minutes." That's Rubyzin on the radio. She's manning the recovery center.

On emergency power my suit isn't fast, but I'm not far from the recovery center. Thank goodness I passed on the temptation to take a short cut which would have saved me thirty minutes of broken field suit-jumping, and showed me a wonderful vista of a Mars canyon, but taken me well away from the chain of recovery centers dotted between Entry Alpha and Entry Delta. I'm learning!

I get to Charlie 14, pop inside, and plug into its life support. I'm back to full power and full communication. The suit diagnostics confirm that I've suffered a main fuel cell failure and all else on the suit is intact. Then I cool my heels. If this was an entertainment sim, the cart would show up in a minute or so, I'd catch up on game admin stuff while I waited, and when it came I'd be fixed on the spot in seconds and then be on my way to the next adventure.

But this is not an entertainment sim. It's not even an educational one. This is the MST final test sim. I can switch on some music, and I can communicate, but I have to wait for that fool rescue cart to actually drive over sim terrain to get here! That'll be in about thirty minutes. Then I have to decide if I want to risk finishing the trip with just a main fuel cell swap, or play it safe and take a ride in the cart back to Entry Alpha and finish this jaunt some other time. It will be my call, and I will make that call after I double check by running some suit diagnostics using equipment that's on the repair cart.

Speaking of… should I remind Ruby to be sure that suit diagnostic equipment is on the cart?… No. It's her job to know that. If I bring it up, I'm being a worrywart. That won't help my personal score any more than being fool-hearty would, and it would hurt the club score. Part of what we are being scored on is how well we work as a team. Instead, I while away my time watching what other team members are doing. On Mars, that's OK to do. It's not considered snooping.

Ruby is in the Rescue Center. It's her shift there. We all take turns at that. We cross-train a lot. Now that she's ordered out the rescue cart, things are quiet again, and she's working on a new dance routine. I laugh to myself—all the Rescue Center is her stage.

Adrian is in the hydroponics area. He's tending there. He and George-776 have been interested in Mars biology since we started on the MAT. Personally, I'm expecting some billion-dollar breakthrough, but that's just because I've been very impressed with what Adrian and George like to work on ever since he took me to his workshop.

Janet is resting and Ben is working on imprinting algorithms for creations that will initiate here on Mars. He is designing their first impressions.… Listen to me! Thinking I'm on Mars already! I guess this sim is doing that part of its job just fine. And I admit, the more I've been working on this project, the more excited I've become to take that big rocket into the sky.

Jaden and Jaina are both working in the Mars babies kindergartens. I notice that they seem to be getting along real well together these days. That's good.

Annette is with us, too. Technically, she's with her Zion on Mars Colony Club, but she's picked up a liaison role, so she's participating in MST's for both groups.

There have been some serious hiccups getting the ZOM's qualified. Individually, the colonists don't pass the means test, and they don't have qualifying education as it is currently defined. Anton has been working closely with Isaac Jesper, the prophet, and the Space Agency colony club bureaucrats to get these two groups coordinated. Getting the ZOM's qualified looks like it will take a few months longer than getting us qualified, and they are going through a whole lot of intensive sim/avatar/creation training in addition to the MAT training. Annette is going to have to decide which group she wants to travel with. When I've talked with her, she seems excited enough about this that she's likely to vote for being part of the advance party, us.

Andy is walking back from lunch. I'm working with him on a geo-survey. That's why I'm out here on the surface. This isn't serious enough to interrupt his meal—when he gets back to his post, he'll find out about my glitch, and we'll talk about what to do next. I'll still be here. Sigh!

"Dahlia! You OK?" It's Andy. He's back and at his console.

"Doing fine. Had a fuel cell failure. I'll head on if I get a green light on the diagnostics from the repair cart."

"Have you checked on the weather? Annette tells me there's a storm coming, a big one."

"What's the ETA? I'm closer to Delta now."

"Let me check…"

Annette gets on the comm link, "Dahlia, Andy, it's big and it will stay a while—hours to a day. It's big enough that the wrong gust in the wrong place will blow the cart over."

"Will some extra weight help stabilize it? My weight?"

"It should," says Andy.

"OK... How about I ride the cart to Delta. It's downwind."

Ruby says, "That rescue vehicle is stationed out of Alpha, but given the circumstances, your plan sounds great. We can move the cart back when the storm ends."

The dust is already kicking up when the cart arrives. I take care to put on the dust cover before I switch fuel cells. I don't take the time to run cart diagnostics. This wind issue is more important. Instead I hop on the cart and head for Delta as lickity-split as the cart will go.

The ride gets wild. Mars' atmosphere is thin, way thinner than Earth's even at the top of Everest, and it blows fast. Hurricane speed winds are a breeze on Mars. So when there is a normal dust storm, there is a little push and a lot of dust blasting—surfaces wear down. But really strong storms can push too. Get in a canyon with a wind howling down and you'll definitely get a push. That's what I'm dodging now.

The visibility is also way down, of course, but that's less of an issue.

Whoa! Then there's the problem of new, very soft, dust dunes! I run right into one! I get off the cart and push it back ten feet, hop on again, and skirt the dune.

Delta Lock is starting to fill with dust, but I get in. This is one of the unsolved problems on Mars: How to keep lock entrances—lee areas—from filling up with dust. Currently, we simply dredge them out in between storms, but there should be a better way.

I stow the cart in the parking area, take off my suit and put it in the cleaner, then report into the receptionist at Delta.

As I do that, the sim dissolves around me. I'm back in my body. I get up, freshen up a bit, and head back to the briefing room where we club members started this MST test. We small talk as we await the results.

The MST coordinator comes in, and she has a genuine smile on her face. She was also quite hospitable during the briefing that started us off. My conclusion: This is no DMV department—the Space Agency really wants to attract well-qualified people to this program.

She takes a final look at her results form and tells us, "In a word… well done, folks. You clearly did your homework.

"Your club qualifies, and you may now pick berth space and start packing."

I'm relieved. This experience has gone much better than I expected. The Space Agency people we've dealt with have all been friendly and the paperwork straightforward—we haven't had to go through much hazing or hoop-jumping.

I'm surprised because this means the Space Agency hasn't had to do a lot of weeding out of the hopeful-but-hopeless. This hasn't been at all like becoming a Hollywood movie star. I'm surprised because this means that going to Mars no longer fires the imagination of a lot of people. In my grandmother's day, people of all walks of life would have lined up around the block for a chance like this. How times have changed. How people's thinking has changed!

Chapter Sixteen

Mars Isn't Earth

Our colony club is not the first group of people to set foot on Mars, far from the first. There have been thirty years of explorers and exploiters and ten years of tourists ahead of us. We are not building the first log cabin in an uncharted wilderness. We are not putting in the first road between unnamed Point A and unnamed Point B. There is lots of human-supporting infrastructure here on Mars already. But we *are* in the first wave of people coming to Mars to stay—to make it a home—and that makes a difference.

Also, these are modern times. There is a lot of creation infrastructure in place on Mars at our beck and call. And we can talk to that infrastructure from Earth, so we can get a lot started long before we arrive. There is the ten minutes-to-couple hours communication delay because Mars is not on Earth, and that was disconcerting at first, but we quickly got used to it.

As soon as we passed the MST, we started planning our habitations and work projects on Mars and started the creations there on implementation. A lot was in place, but a lot still had to be done.

The trip over is routine. We pack, we get on transports that take us to orbit over Earth, we transfer to the Mars Shuttle—the newer faster one—and we take two months to get there traveling at a steady .05G the whole way. .05G is enough to keep us from floating around like you do on an orbiting space station, and there is a definite sense of up and down on this ship. But it sure isn't Earth—we do bounce around like we have super powers. And sadly, Ben, Janet and Miranda's mother have a hard time. They take drugs and mope a bit the whole way—they may be young at heart, but their real hearts and bodies still have some old parts and are having a hard time adapting. Even with all the regeneration technology we have these days, hormonal secondary feedback systems are devilishly hard to keep in balance.

We arrive, get on Mars transports, and land. One-third G felt positively heavy for a few days! We do a bit of processing, all of five minutes—it's not like we could have come from somewhere strange. We stay in the main tourist hotel, The South Pole Mars Marriott, the first night.

The next day our on-Mars orientation starts, and it starts with a trip outside. "You aren't likely to be doing this often, but you should at least do it once so the wonder gets out of your system," Mary Lou, our hostess, informed us. We bundle up three at a time and with a host shepherd go out on the "playground". Part of it is a playground, and we get to do things such as such as swinging and sliding and climbing around on jungle gyms. Part of it is some rough terrain—a gully with windswept gravel on top, cliff sides, and dust dunes in the bottom. We feel what it is like to navigate those in person. In the low G and with the suit assist, I feel like an Olympic-class gorilla. I am a-jumpin and a-swingin and a-lopin all over the place. It's a blast!

The suits are rugged, so taking a tumble is not an issue. The issue is just being sure to monitor the suit's condition. If things do get out of whack, conditions inside can get unpleasant real quickly. That I learned from the MST.

And then (Sigh!) we feel what it is like to clean our stuff up when we finish and come inside. Some of that dust has its surface ionized by the UV in the sunlight and it gets real sticky.

After we finish our outdoor initiation and clean up, we meet with Skyler Abercromby and Phil-422, the administrators on Mars who will be handling colony affairs until we set up a colonial government, and there is a hand-off.

Skyler begins, "So... you folks are going to be staying here. Well, Mars isn't Earth, so I guess you folks are no longer Earthlings, are you?" he grins.

"But you're not Martians yet. Right now, you're Martian wannabes. You're something that neither I nor my people want to be: We're Earthlings a long way from home. You're wannabes because you're not experienced enough to be full Martians. My job, my goal in this project, is to get you experienced as fast as I can. Phil-422 will be helping me on that.

Adrian raises his hand, "When will we be full Martians?"

"We've been working over the criteria for that. I believe our memo on that has been sent to your club."

I nod. It has.

"Basically, when your group can handle the various emergencies and crises that come up here as well as my engineers can, then you're official Martians. It's as simple as that at this point."

"Sounds surprisingly simple," says Adrian.

"It does to me, too, Mr. Messenger. I think that's because there aren't dozens of people lining up three deep for these slots. The Space Agency can still keep it simple.

"If you find the hidden caves filled with Martian gold that we transients haven't found, and people do start lining up, then the initiation may get tougher. But for now, you have the virtue of being first in a venture that is only modestly interesting to people on Earth."

Phil-442 interrupts, "It is only modestly interesting to the *people* of Earth, but it is quite interesting to the *creations*. We want this to go well."

The rest of the meeting concerns administrative details.

< < < * > > >

One thing that is high on our early priority list is finishing our accommodations. We are not tourists, we are worker bees, so our designs emphasize accessibility to tools and work areas, not luxury, safety, and entertainment. They also emphasize flexibility—our jobs will change as we complete projects and start on new ones. The good news is that because we have been in constant communication with the Mars construction contractors, there are few surprises in what we find when we get here.

Our plans add something entirely new to Mars infrastructure: areas for children and child raising. This is something we are all interested in, but Jaina and Annette—yes, Annette came with us—take the lead here. As the incubators and kindergartens are completed, the Earth governments will start moving new Mars baby-making activities to the planet, and the existing programs on Earth will be directed towards making other kinds of odd... I mean non-standard... babies.

The designs we humans wanted for these areas put us at odds with the creation infrastructure on Mars. Our designs emphasize "teach"; their designs emphasize "safe". Their proposed designs put the child care in the deepest parts of the habitable infrastructure. We veto that—they would be high, so the kids can learn and experience.

"We aren't raising Morlocks," I grumble to Phil-422.

Jaden takes up the project of documenting everything we do. We all learn to expect his second question when he comes visiting, "Care to explain what you're up to to an audience?" He gets pretty good at prepping us with talking points and asking good questions when the recording starts. And he gets good at cultivating distributors and show producers back on Earth. We get a respectable amount of air time, and interest in the project is rising. He also sends shivers up the creations' spines: He proposes and starts outlining a series of hiking trails up top that go to nearby scenic vistas and other points of interest. The creations feel that everything interesting on Mars should be manufactured and placed in some kind of cavern.

"You want to go outside? You can sim that," they argue, but we humans insist that getting outside will be a common Martian experience. We order up a lot more topside infrastructure and access points.

"This is adding considerable danger," they caution, but then comply.

Adrian and Ruby get about finding more things that Martians can make that Earthlings will want to buy. Ruby splits her time between coordinating with Adrian and producing her own "value-add-in" entertainment projects. I split my time between helping Ruby on entertainment, helping Jaina and Annette on kid stuff, and creating "Red Planet Originals" fashions.

The Red Planet Originals capture the spirit of Mars. The first generation designs are red, and in retrospect, suck eggs in my eyes. But they turn out to be popular on Earth because of the curiosity factor and because my thinking is still very Earth harmonious. What I do to improve my subsequent generations of designs is monitor closely what Jaden is documenting. That is connecting me to my inner Mars muse. The second generation stuff is high-fashioned versions of environmental suits and leisure wear that is better suited to low-G and tunnel environments. At first these don't sell as well, but as Jaden's documentaries get more popular, so do my newer creations. They come to be seen as genuine.

And whew! I am busy! But in truth, we all are. There is so much to do here!

Well… almost all of us. Ben and Janet are not as busy as the rest of us. It isn't that they don't want to be, but their bodies are just not adapting well to Mars conditions. They start spending a lot of time in an Earth-G centrifuge at the Marriott and doing things through their avatars. It is expensive, and it takes some getting used to seeing them mostly in avatar form, but they don't get discouraged. They pitch right in, and we get used to it. Thankfully Miranda's mom adapts and with time she feels much better than Ben and Janet. The human body is still full of surprises.

Anton stayed on Earth. He is working on keeping the immigrant queue full. One project that helps that is coordinating with Jaden to get his documentaries distributed.

George-776 came with us and continues to work with Adrian—there are howls at the expense of doing that, but the club backs them up. We know how tight they are. The rest of us pick up new assistants here on Mars, and those new assistants pull up lots of history from our Earth assistants, so they are up to speed on both us and Mars conditions.

The Honeymoon Ends

We constantly run into the issue that we never have the right or enough resources to accomplish what we feel is high priority. The creation infrastructure expects us to act like long-term tourists, but we are here to change the world! So we want to do new things, things tourists don't do. It's the difference between building a Disneyland and a factory.

When it is just a matter of ordering in new equipment from Earth, we don't get too much flack, unless it is really expensive new equipment because it is heavy or bulky. Each time the heavy/bulky issue comes up, we backtrack a bit and look at what equipment and expertise it would take to make the heavy and bulky here, then we place an order for that. That doesn't cause as much hardship with the existing infrastructure boys. They recognize that making stuff is why we are here, and the extractor people are already heavy into the making-stuff mode.

But the honeymoon ends as we start developing distinctively Martian ways of doing things, such as child raising and recreating. Some of these look needlessly dangerous to the creation powers-that-be, and they object.

The child-raising issues come up first. It starts while we are still on Earth when we colonists propose the child-raising areas be up top. It comes to a head when the Zion Club arrives and the creations see how the Zion Club child raisers are actually organizing the child caring areas. They begin implementing their Mars-version of the wild-and-wooly child-raising antics they'd been getting away with on Earth.... Or so it seems to the Mars creations who are getting involved, and, I admit, some of us city-bred on-lookers.

Annette and I have a meeting with Skyler and Phil-422. Skyler called the meeting, and Annette tells me about the issues being brought up and asks me to come along for moral support.

At the meeting, Phil-422 opens the main issue, "Mrs. Bushkov, the creation command structure your club is asking for is causing us great concern. You really want *children* commanding the creations? This can go wrong in so many ways."

"That we do," she replies.

Skyler jumps in, "Mrs. Bushkov, I took the opportunity to

review your club's history. On Earth you folks were quite... creation resistant, is that not so?"

"That's true. We feel that humankind should do as much for itself as it can. We felt that creations—creation help, that is—represented temptation. We should use them only in moderation... great moderation."

"But here on Mars you seem to be embracing them fully?"

"One of the decisions our group's leadership made before we decided to embark on the emigrating process was that here on Mars creations should be considered a full part of the human tool kit, not a temptation for humans to do less than they should, as they are on Earth. As the saying goes, Mars is not Earth."

"Phil-422 tells me that the adult use of creations has been a bit clumsy. There have been accidents, avoidable accidents."

Annette squirms a bit—this is not news to her. "We Zionists are learning, Mr. Abercromby. In this we are much like our children, and this is why we wish them to have much control over the creations. This is how they will learn quickest and best."

"There will be injuries, potentially very serious ones."

"We are aware of that."

"And not just to the person who gives a poorly thought through command."

"The people of Zion are quite aware of the damage accidents cause. We experienced them all the time in our Earthly lifestyle. We feel the benefits of understanding and being in command of our fate far outweigh the damages that come from mistakes." She says this with the confidence of faith.

Skyler looks at me.

I say, "I've seen the Zion Club operate on Earth. It's strange for me to watch, and a bit spooky. I wouldn't want to live that way, but I support their being able to do things the way they wish to."

"You realize that you could suffer damage too? That we all could."

"I recognize that. I recognize there should be limits. But I also recognize that there are likely to be benefits as well—big, surprise benefits."

He looks at Phil-422.

"Let us integrate a training program into the handing-over process, and let us include adults in that training program."

The meeting covers a few more details and then breaks up. The child care area is soon filled with odd construction projects that the kids are thinking up, and the accident rate with Zion Club usage of creations drops steadily.

< < < * > > >

The rearranging of child-raising areas is just the start. The proposal to have the Sierra Pit Barsoom Platter Race precipitates another full-blown, formal meeting.

A “Bar plat”, short for Barsoom platters, is a simple, flat, round metal platter some four feet across. You plop it down on some of the seasonal dry-ice cake that builds up over the winter on the surface at the poles. (Our base, the main base on Mars, is near the south pole where there is lots of water ice available for us to extract for life support.) When that platter is heated a bit by spring sunlight, or by putting a heater on it, or pointing a big light at it, the CO2 underneath will sublime and the platter starts shaking and shimmering and acting like a man-size air puck, complete with lots of hissing and spitting noises and mist and dust squirting out around the edges—quite an experience—and it gets louder and more agitated the heavier the weight. When a person hops on, it screams like a banshee and starts heading off in one direction or another. Riding it is like a surf board, except you can go any direction, and fall off in any direction when it gets ahead of you, or when it bounces as it hits a bump, or stops dead on a rock or some not-slippery grit or water ice. Wee!! It is a ride!

Bar plattering is a seasonal event. The fresh CO2 surface, the non-gritty kind, gathers in steadily in the winter and burns off in late spring. During the dark nights of winter and early spring it is just too cold! So this is a distinctively Martian return-of-spring rite, and we want to make it just that—sort of like the Iditarod sled race in Alaska.

Adrian and Jaden first got a chance to do this when they went with some extractors to visit North Pole base. And Jaden got the bright idea of making a contest and documenting it when spring rolled around at South Pole. But when word of his hot idea started spreading, the line in the red dust was crossed. A meeting is called.

Skyler calls the meeting to order and gets straight to the point. "An outdoor race? You can sim that! Why not just use the tourist facilities for your recreation? There is available capacity, and all us transients use those all the time."

The last statement is... well, not quite entirely true. We colonials have been shown a few gray area tricks early on by grizzled extractor types we've become drinking buddies with. We are simply adding to the repertoire of what is cool but not conventional and being more open about it—and perhaps a little sillier. We are still the rookies here, as this Bar platter race idea demonstrates.

"Do you realize the infrastructure you're calling for?" chides Skyler. "This means suits appropriate for hours-at-a-time outdoor stays, not just hour-max like we have now. So a full suit redesign. Plus some kind of pressurized tent, or a tunnel plus high-capacity entrance so you can move a crowd in and out quickly and safely. This isn't just about whipping up a few more Barsoom platters, this is huge."

Well... yeah... it is big. We take a few moments to think and look amongst ourselves, and reaffirm.

I speak for the group. "It's big. But it's Martian. Yes, we want to invest in this."

Skyler shakes his head in resignation, consults for a moment with Phil-422, then says, "Well, it's not as big as opening a new mine. Get me a detailed proposal."

Chapter Seventeen

The Constitution

Nine months after our landing, Ben and Janet call and ask me for a face-to-face. We set up a time and I head for the Marriott to meet them in the restaurant. They greet me as I come in. They are looking thin and move like they are weary, but there is a brightness in their eyes that says they've made some kind of happy choice.

"You're looking well," I lie after I order. Their hard time adapting is something unsettling. They've been trying many different things, and we've all been watching, expecting a breakthrough, but nothing has completed their adaptation to this Mars environment. I guess there are still medical miracles we can't accomplish.

"We've made a choice, and that's half of what we wanted to talk to you about," says Ben,

"but before we get to that, we need to talk about a Mars colonial government."

I admit it—I've been so busy, that topic has slipped my mind. "I guess we should. Our relation with Skyler has been going so smoothly I haven't given much thought to a formal government."

"I agree, but now is the time, when things look good. When the crisis comes, choices will get hasty.... And there will be a crisis. There always is when large groups are working towards an uncertain goal.

"Janet and I have been giving this a lot of thought, and we'll be happy to pass those thoughts on to you and the others, but that brings up the second issue."

Ben pauses and looks at Janet for confirmation. She nods.

"Janet and I are sending our bodies back to Earth. They are just not hacking it here.

"But… we will stay here as cybers, and then we'll inhabit some specially designed human bodies when those become available. They will be both designed for Mars and designed to mesh transparently with a cyber consciousness. Our new bodies are being grown right now in Austin. Well… were, they will be part of the first shipment of Mars babies being sent here. They will be ready to begin the cyber meshing in about three years, and it will take about nine years for their minds to develop to the point that a full mesh with an adult cyber will be comfortable. When they get to about age twelve they will become us."

My jaw drops, "Has the technology come that far?"

Janet continues for Ben, "Just barely. We and Anton pulled some strings, and we will be among the first."

Ben goes on, "It's breakthrough stuff, so there are likely to be some surprise minuses as well as the known pluses. Worst case: we have to go back to square one a couple times. But if we want to be full contributors to this Mars colony, and we do, we feel a step like this is necessary."

Janet says, "This meshing process will take a lot of our attention. So for a few years we will be… distracted, I guess is the best way to put it. We'll be around as avatars, but not with whole mind."

This is such a surprise it takes a while before I say, "When will this happen?"

"We would like to see this government-making project solidly in the queue before we start the transition… but we would like to start soon. We really aren't happy with our current state of affairs."

"Specifically, we would like to see a constitutional convention happen—one that we will attend—before we start the transition."

We finish lunch and I pass the news on, and thus it is that

perhaps we will have "founding persons of our planet" after being on world only twelve months… six months Mars time, that is…. Well, Mars doesn't have a big moon with a leisurely orbit like Earth, so we'll continue to use Earth months, so twelve months. Boy, this being a colonist does have its surprises.

< < < * > > >

Miranda is the first to react to the news, "What about their child!" she exclaims to me. She's right. I'd forgotten about that too. She hurries over to the Marriott and invites me along. The four of us meet in the lobby.

Miranda starts, "I apologize about being so long getting back to you on this, we've all been so busy. I have been thinking about this since the day you proposed it. And the more I think about it, the more comfortable I become." she pauses, then declares, "I really want to help you with your child. I really would." She looks very sincere about this.

Ben and Janet look at each other. Ben starts, "Ever since we've started this journey through space, this has been such a struggle for us." he sighs, "We really haven't felt up to it."

Janet continues, "Now, we have this new challenge facing us. I just don't see how we can do justice to any child we start now."

She says this, but both she and Bob are looking as unhappy as I've ever seen them look.

Miranda looks back and forth between them, then says, "This is a burden you don't have to carry alone. Let me help you. You have helped me so much. Let me help you now."

"And me," I added, "You have helped all of us. Helping each other is what Child Champs is all about." and I add in deep earnest, "That's not just some kind of slogan any more. This is for real. We all want you to make this dream happen."

Ben and Janet look at each other. And they straighten up a bit. Janet takes Miranda by her hand, "Thank you, dear. I would say that you have no idea how much this means to us, but you clearly do," she looks at me as well, "You all do."

Ben says, "Tomorrow we will begin preparations for starting

our new child with Miranda's help. Once again, thank you, thank you, thank you."

< < < * > > >

When I bring up the constitutional convention with Skyler, he gives me a "Yes, but..." back.

"Yes, we should have one, but there's a new group of colonists already en route. They are from China, and I think it would be good to have them in on this."

I have to agree the diversity would be good. The convention is scheduled for three months later, and the Chinese clubs are informed that, rookie though they will be, they will participate. Ben and Janet take the news stoically, and we all stay busy.

Along with the Chinese immigrants come the Mars babies that the Austin facility has been raising. Those from the other labs will come on later flights. Actually, the oldest are full-fledged children now, attending forth grade. We all gather to welcome the newcomers—all of them—and Jaina and Annette hustle the Mars kids off to our newly-built facilities, and there we introduce foster parents. The Chinese clubs are bringing a lot of kids with them. They and the Zion Club now split most of the child raising space between them. The Child Champs club picks up four: Cindy, Marge, Alex, and Russell, and takes technical custody of the Ben and Janet mesh babies, called "Bens and Janets". There are six of them because this is still a very uncertain process and they take some very special raising that is mostly creation-handled.

With the arrival of the Mars babies, we see a tangible symbol of our future humanity here on Mars. We now have to set up two different Martian environments: one for the transplanted Earthlings such as us, and one for the more acclimated Martians such as the Mars babies are. Yes, it's disconcerting, but we are all so busy that the strangeness quickly becomes toleration. Mars isn't Earth.

I have lunch with Annette one day after the Mars babies arrive and ask her how the Zion Club feels about the Mars babies. She says the jury is still out in their group. Some feel this is just another element in the strangeness, and some feel this is even more of an abomination than Geishas. But like everyone else, they are all so busy that it is an issue for another time. The compromise is that Zion Club members will not be tending any of the Mars babies from this batch. They will wait and see.

"I'm hopeful that we will be taking our share of the next batch," she says. "We all know these kids are going to be a big part of Mars' future. It's just some more strangeness we have to get over."

But the new crop of Earth-adapted babies from the newly arriving clubs brings out another honeymoon breaker: How to raise the kids. There is just one facility for all the kids at this point, so we all get to see each others' techniques. And with all of us being full of human instinct, we start kibitzing about what we see.

The Chinese want a very organized environment. They plan carefully what their children will learn and don't want to waste much time with unstructured activities. They are quite willing to devote a lot of personal attention—human and cyber—to each child, and each child has a carefully organized program. That calls for a child-raising facility with lots of classrooms, very organized play areas, and child-tending creations who are controlled mostly by the parents.

As I mentioned earlier, the Zioners want a real world environment for their kids. They are quite willing to give the kids time to learn on their own, as well as having organized class time. And they also want the kids interacting with parents and creations who are doing real world activities—apprenticing in its oldest form. They feel that learning by experience and example is the best way for the kids to learn what is important. They have workshops near the child-raising areas and play areas with lots of materials for building stuff, and they let the tending creations take orders from the kids—not crazy ones, mind you, that had been worked out, but the kids are learning early on how to integrate creations into their project-building activities.

We at Child Champs want our kids to have the best too, but that brings us to our own internal honeymoon breaker. Jaina starts spending time with the kids right from the start, which is good since the rest of us are getting busy in so many other ways. But she is young and so enthusiastic that she turns into a by-the-training-book enthusiast. She is constantly reading the latest, from Earth authors since there are no Mars authors on this topic yet, and then enthusiastically trying to apply it. And she hasn't fully caught on to the Mars isn't Earth concept. In fact, I find some of what she is saying and proposing downright spooky in its naivety. Because it is written so much about, she is buying fully into the children-must-be-protected doctrine that is raging among Earth media people that cover child raising.

I talk with Miranda and suggest she and her family get involved. When she does, that brings the raising-style issue to a sharp climax. The specific issue is Jaina forbidding our kids from playing with Zion Club kids. She says the setting is too dangerous. I set up a meeting with Jaina, Miranda, and myself.

Jaina comes in sullen and Miranda exasperated.

"I don't see what the problem is," says Jaina. "I'm reading up and I'm doing exactly what the best child-raising articles recommend."

"You're doing that exceedingly well," I say. I look at Miranda and she says nothing. She is falling back on her culture's ways which are very careful about critisism and confrontation.

"What's this I hear about keeping the kids away from the Zion Club kids?" I ask.

Jaina is quick and prescriptive. "Those kids are engaging in dangerous activities. They are going to get hurt. I don't want our kids hurt."

I look at her. "You realize we are on Mars now?" and look some more.

"Yes..."

"Have you been outside?"

"Not since the initiation."

"Have you been to Hydroponics?"

"No."

"Have you been to the tea garden the Chinese are setting up in Chinatown?"

"No! I've been with the kids. I love being with the kids! What's the point of this third degree?"

"The point is that there's more to Mars than a kindergarten. If you're going to teach kids how to live on Mars, I think you need to have a better idea of what's going on here."

"Well, I've been pretty busy.... How do you propose I do that?"

"I propose that you spend a month as Jaden's assistant while he's doing his documentaries. He really needs the help, and you will get to see what's going on outside the kindergarten."

"Who will take care of the kids?"

"Miranda and her family."

Jaina looks sharply at Miranda. She is clearly not happy hearing that. With effort, Miranda gets out of her old culture rut and stares back, locking eyes, daring her.

"Are... are...?" Thank goodness Jaina's good sense kicks in before some snappy retort comes out. Her face relaxes, "... I guess you did pass the PAT's on the first try." She gives us both a smile of concession, "OK. I'll give Jaden a shout."

"He's working on some interesting stuff. You'll have a good time," I assure her. And it's true. We are all working on interesting stuff.

With Miranda now in the lead, we start with a Chinese-style approach with lots of planning and personal attention. But we want kids with a more artistic side, and getting that means loosening up on the planning and letting the kids get more experimental, a little more Zionish. It isn't apprenticeship like the Zions, and it isn't regimentation like the Chinese, it is a Child Champs approach, Mars version.

What we all find is that we really can get deep into our different approaches. There is kibitzing, but no censuring.

What we *all* agree on is that the kids should be exposed to risk—this is a place where skinned knees, broken bones, and even potential death has to be part of the environment. Mars is not Earth.

< < < * > > >

Which brings us back to the constitution, and with it, the legal system.

I worry that this constitution project will suffer deeply from the Curse of Being Important—that everyone will have an opinion, and we'll end up with a many chefs and spoiled broth situation. And in fact, everyone does have an opinion. The amount of blogging and other forms of gossiping about the constitution leading up to the convention is perhaps ten percent of the inter-club communication. But to my surprise, everyone is willing to delegate—each club nominates delegates and the convention is convened. It is held at the Marriott where Ben and Janet are staying, and they and Skyler and Kim ManDoo from one of the Chinese clubs formed the executive committee. Ben and Janet are elder statespeople by every definition, Kim ManDoo is a well-traveled businessperson who as a young man also participated in China's governmental revolution of the 2060s, and Skyler has had plenty of practice representing on-Mars transients' interests. George-776 and Phil-422 represent the creation interests.

We've come a long way from 1787, in the case of the US, and 2063, in the case of China, so there are going to be some big differences. All through the 21st century, there has been a lot of thinking and research done about how to organize social systems, and now we have creations to add to the social mix as well as all the Information Age communication and computational tools. Plus, now we have a chance for a fresh start.

The first decision, made early on, is that we won't attempt any sort of mix-and-match from the existing US and Chinese legal systems. Both systems are now way overgrown and too adapted to Earthly conditions and traditions. We can use the tabula rasa here, the clean slate, and we will. We go back to the basics of what a legal system should do and build up using modern concepts supported with modern technology and adapted to Mars' conditions. Whew! It is a lot to ask. The good news is it is all talk, and these days we can do that really quickly.

The delegates take their responsibilities seriously and refrain from taking cheap shots... well, not too many, anyway. And all the colonials support them being responsible. We are all here by choice, we are all new to this wonderful opportunity, and we're all going to be living with this for a long time, so we don't want to screw it up.

The document that emerges is a sparse one, like the US constitution. It lays ground rules and does not get into micromanaging details and the hot issues de jour. The two guiding lights are keeping citizens enfranchised and avoiding panic-and-blunder decision making.

The former means recognizing that supporting minority rights and opinions is as vital as supporting majority rights and opinions—not in the brittle, prescriptive, and intolerant sense that the American politically correct version of tolerance soured into in the early 21st century, but in the live-and-let-live sense of the immigrant-flooded cities of late 19th century America and late 20th century Hong Kong.

The latter means structuring decision-making so that choices are made with cost-benefit in mind as well as emotional heat, and that making cool-headed revisions some time later becomes a recognized part of the decision-making process, not something exceptional or threatening to those who make the decisions of the moment. This is the modern-day implementation of the checks and balances of the US constitution. This new system includes creation participation in the decision-making process. They will take on the role of being the cool heads.

And both tenets mean that keeping human citizens informed and governing transparent are essential to making and supporting good choices.

The constitution concerns itself mostly with making an enforceable legal foundation. There will be rule of law, and the laws enacted will be both respectful and enforceable. This is the 22nd century: Separating church and state is not a hot topic in our time, but there will be an article concerning the separation of legality and morality—no busybody laws. Everyone agrees that this is a hot topic de jour, but even so we will include a provision on it in this constitution.

The constitution says very little about administration. These modern-day founders wisely recognize that administration will change wildly as Mars grows in population and as its purpose in the solar system evolves. Thanks in large part to Kim ManDoo's input and his experience with the Chinese constitution, this is written as a document that should not be ignored or reinterpreted when heat-of-the-moment expedience suggests it should be.

In addition to the legal foundation it also covers money carefully: How the government can tax. And here the Curse does get strong: Every colonist has an opinion on how the government should be financed.... And so do the extractors, and tourists, and people on Earth who are following colony affairs! Deciding money issues actually takes up most of the convention time, and here Ben and Janet and ManDoo do their most and best pushing.

It is decided that keeping taxes simple will be a core value: Taxes will not be used for social engineering purposes. As examples, if it is decided that boozing is bad, that will not justify a bigger tax on booze to discourage drinking, and even though saving is a good idea, that will not be an excuse for implementing government-controlled/supported/sponsored savings programs such as mandatory pensions. Social engineering will be handled by other means, not by the government making new kinds of taxes or other financing schemes.

This is a long and tough fight for the trio. There are endless streams of "Yes, but's..." offered by well-meaning advocacy groups from all the clubs and even across club boundaries—and from Earth—but in the end the trio prevail, and tax simplicity is written into the constitution in unambiguous terms.

Even with modern communication and computation, it takes three months of serious talking and negotiation to put this document together. The constitution is ratified a month after it is finished, and a month after that, Ben and Janet begin their cyber transformation, and Miranda's belly is just noticeably swelling.

And all the while this is going on, the rest of us are busy bees as well.

Busy Bees

Adrian and George start a new workshop. They populate this one quickly. Yes, the fruit flies are back, but when I visit I find that Adrian has a new favorite toy.

"Martian nanobots!" he proclaims. "These are white hot... well red hot, I guess." He grins, George-776 groans. "This cool, bone-dry, UV-flooded environment changes efficient nanobot parameters. UV provides a higher energy potential. It can directly power many carbon-related covalent bonding changes—they don't call it ionizing radiation for no reason. The bone-dry means we can mix in a lot of metal catalyst sites on the molecules we build up. On Earth the water molecules would latch on to those and break them up in a microsecond. The cool promotes energy radiating efficiency. This is a whole new ball game!"

"We may even come up with some formidable Mars climate-changing technologies," adds George-776. "Compared to Earth's diversity of climates and organics, Mars is an unwritten-upon whiteboard. The whole surface has only a handful of climates and surface minerals. If a technique works in one place, it is likely to work over much of the planet, and with only a handful of techniques, the entire planetary climate can be changed."

By the end of my visit, I am getting envious. I make a resolution to keep in touch with Adrian more often.... He might have some free time, and Mars isn't Earth.

I find Ruby is spending an hour a day outside. She invites me along for a session. When we get outside, she takes me to a scenic spot and goes into a dance routine. It looks different than anything I've seen done before. It is a bit... eerie. She finishes and we talk.

"This scenery, this alien environment, has been inspiring," she says.

"If you come here often, should we install a rescue chamber?" I say. I am thinking of my MST experience.

She laughs, "Not needed. I change my location frequently, and the creations know I'm out here."

I relax and get into her moment. "I admit, those are moves I've never seen before. They were... unsettling, I guess is the best way to put it."

"Yeah. They look different and feel different to execute. Mars changes the human performance playbook. Now that I'm moving beyond being a tourist here, I'm getting excited about this potential to show off something new." She looks at me and waits, like there is something profound in what she is saying.

At first I don't see it, then the Ah-Hah! hits me, and I get even more into her moment. "You're right. This is original. Truly original! Not Hollywood- or Broadway-style recycled from fifty years ago original."

"I'm working up routines and techniques. And this is something to both show off personally and build up a school around."

"Jaden?"

She nods, "A once-in-a-lifetime opportunity. I hope he's up to it."

"He should be, but if he's not, there will be others. The colony is growing."

Ruby—and likely Jaden—have found their Martian paradise. And I can help, too—they will be needing Martian-inspired costuming. Something that combines beauty with a pressure suit. Hmm...

< < < * > > >

Jaden is also working on a project with Andy. Andy is a kid in a candy shop with all this new scenery. He'd already spent hours and hours looking at satellite and drone views. Now he is here in person. At first he spent hours in a drone he personally remote piloted. As he was doing this, he had the creations design a man-piloted scout craft. This is another project that got Skyler and Phil-422 face-palming, and another meeting is called.

"You want what? A manned scout? You realize that it's not just the scout vessel you're asking for, it's all the infrastructure and safety back up. We will need at least two, probably three, vessels plus some kind of rescue/repair vessel and system. This is why we use drones and avatars, to keep the expense down.

"And you want to scout where? Tharsis area? Christ! That's the equator, son. You can't get farther from existing human habitation than that! Unless you're going for a sub-orbital flyover, it's hours just to get there, and you want to dawdle and nose around after you arrive? You're talking some sort of supplied sub-base... still more expensive infrastructure." He sighs.

"That's not the worst of what I'm going to be asking for," replies Andy confidently. "Once I have scouted the area personally, I will be proposing we set up a five-star Tharsis resort."

Yes, Skyler's jaw does drop a bit. Andy continues.

"The Tharsis area is home to Olympus Mons, Mars' three other huge volcanoes, and Valles Marineris, the solar system's largest canyon. This is a place people—Earth people as well as Mars people—are going to want to experience first-hand. There's a ton of tourist money to be made there."

Skyler is speechless. Part of that is his pausing to let his cyber side absorb the proposal that Andy's cyber infrastructure has assembled and put on the net.

"... Well, you've come up with something that's bigger than building a mine here. In fact, it's a hundred times building a mine. Which means it's well beyond my ability to authorize. This project is one that's going to wait until you've got a government, and that government has access to credit, lots of credit." He grins, "I think that constitution we are working on is going to get put to use pretty quickly.

"In the meantime, I can authorize a short-range, human-piloted, drone STOL—short take off and landing—prototype project. You can get your feet wet exploring the South Pole here personally."

The design of the scout proceeds quickly. It is done in a month, and after a bit of thinking-through, made a two-seater, not single. While Andy is working on that, I am working on an appropriate suit. This puts us together a lot, and as the month goes on I notice Andy acting a bit... strange... when we are together in person. He is getting really up, even silly at times. I notice I am comfortable with him when he gets that way. I start laughing a lot.

And... it happens. After the first test flight, he invites me to the Marriott for dinner, and over dinner takes my hand and says, "Dahl... I've been thinking. Thinking a lot. I'm feeling good about Mars and my life here. And... I'm ready. I want some children to share these good times with me. I know you used to be interested in me... and in doing that with me. Are you still interested? If you are, I'm interested. I'm very interested now." He looks deep into my eyes.

What can I say? He was a good choice back on Earth. He is an even better choice now! Yeah, my life has changed a lot—his life has changed a lot. We are both terribly busy. But...

I move my chair next to his and cuddle him and give him a big, long kiss. Then we finish our dinner side-by-side. It looks totally crazy in a classy place like the Marriott. But… Mars isn't Earth, and I don't feel so walking-on-sunshine very often. I wonder if there are "remember him" pills… but then again, I won't need any!

We are not alone in getting baby-making heat. Over the next few months, Ruby and Adrian announced and, to my surprise, Jaina finds herself Yang ZeDong, a wonderful Chinese man. Not quite so surprising is so does Miranda…. Yeah, getting them both some out-of-nursery time is working wonders.

Chapter Eighteen

No Nukes on Mars!

Over the next year, between marriages and baby-making and more immigration, the Mars colony continues to grow in both population and diversity of activities. And it continues to surprise.

One surprise is that Adrian, Skyler, George-776, and Phil-422 come up with another Tharsis project to rival Andy's resort idea, and this time it is a mining project. Thanks to Andy's scouting around Tharsis, they find commercially valuable concentrations of uranium and cementerium—a distinctly Martian mineral—on two slopes of Arsia Mons, one of the shield volcanoes on the Tharsis. At first their presence in such high concentrations was a mystery. *After* the deposits had been found, an immigrant Argentine geologist explained why they are there.

"The dust on that side of Arsia is created by blasting grains off the basalt which is Arsia's flank. This basalt contains a bit of uranium, as all planetary igneous rocks do, but as part of basalt it's too diffuse to be commercially interesting. But… these grains blasted off the basalt are pushed into dunes by the prevailing wind, and then pushed upslope. But because the dunes are being pushed up a steep slope, they periodically slump back down again. After that happens, the winds reform them and push them upslope again. This goes on over and over, and in the process the uranium-rich grains, being bigger and heavier, slowly collect and concentrate at the bottoms of the dunes. The cementerium grains, being lighter but not smaller, collect in the lee areas on the high side of the dunes. The smaller, lighter particles that are not either just keep flying up and up, over the top, and end up on the plains downwind of the volcano.

"This process is something of a fluke. It takes special circumstances, and it's not going to happen in many places, so we are lucky to have found these examples.... And I'm going to get an honorary degree from somewhere for figuring this out. Thanks, Andy and others, for finding this," he grins, "and where is the line for investing?"

Mineable uranium means nuclear power. Cementerium is the ingredient in Martian dust that makes our suits so hard to clean. It can also be a key component in powerful adhesives which we can export back to Earth.

Cementerium is nice, everyone agrees on that. But nuclear power is something that separates Martians from Earthlings—separates them in a big emotional way. Mars has no fossil fuel; there is no equivalent to oil, coal, or natural gas on Mars. Importing petroleum products such as gasoline makes as much sense as importing water: none at all. Not only is it heavy like water is, it would consume valuable oxygen that has to be manufactured on Mars, and running a gas-powered engine indoors would directly add to life support infrastructure requirements. In a sentence, "No, no, a thousand times no."

So solar power from solar panels is the primary energy source on Mars. Up until this mineable uranium was found, it was essentially the only source. (The other source is imported uranium from Earth.) Solar is a better fit on Mars than on Earth. The atmosphere is thin and there is no ozone, so we get a lot more UV in the solar mix than earth does, and this makes the panels more efficient. The only weather is dust storms which only affect solar intensity—the wind is too thin to blow anything but the finest dust particles around—and the storms are much more predictable than Earth weather. So solar works a bit better than on Earth. But it's not helpful for mobile power—the power that runs cars, planes, and things humans wear.

Batteries are almost as bad to import as gasoline, they are so heavy! (This is one of our first importing lessons we learn as rookies.) Manufacturing them here on Mars is also prohibitively expensive because of the "crustal abundance problem" on Mars. Rare earths and heavy metals on Earth are concentrated into veins by billions of years of plate tectonics and water-dominated weather. Mars has never had plate tectonics and only the briefest eras of water-dominated weather. On Mars "crustal abundance" applies everywhere as far as commercially-interesting Earth-style minerals are concerned. There are no veins. Profitable "mining" on Mars consists of scraping interesting stuff off the surface after it is created by the UV baking.

Prior to exploiting this uranium discovery, the dominant portable energy technology was fuel cells run by hydrogen dissociated from water using solar power. It works, but it is so expensive!

This is why the discovery of uranium being concentrated by the slump dunes on Arsia Mons is so Earth shak… uh, Mars shaking! This is an incredible cheap energy breakthrough! It is a game-changer!

But… on Earth nuclear is still a panic-inducing energy form. Most people, and it seems like every media person, still equate nuclear power and those mushroom cloud pictures of the 1950s. So when we Martians announce that we are about to have a nuclear bonanza, the Earth media freaks out and a lot of human concern is generated. (George-776 tells me the creations quietly applaud the nuclear as a huge cost savings.)

Earth legislators start speechifying that if Mars implements nuclear power, they will require all returning visitors to be checked for radiation contamination. ("And extra heads… both kinds," we Martians mock.)

Mars isn't Earth. We jump into nuclear with both feet.

The surprising part is how quick and simple exploiting nuclear can be! In our Earth existence, nuclear was thought of as only something for making electric power, something that takes huge facilities to use, and something that takes years and years to develop. Here on Mars we learn that most of that cost and construction time is regulation induced. Here on Mars, thanks in part to our new constitution, we find that nuclear power plants can be developed in months, not decades.

That is just the first surprise. The second surprise is how many smaller interesting applications there are! Thousands! Once the genie is let out of the regulatory bottle, there is no end of interesting applications that call for nuclear engines the size of car engines, and even the size of rice grains. And they are good applications!

Nuclear is so good it starts getting really strange—strange-frightening to some and strange-wonderful to others. It is getting so popular that we are requesting even more uranium imports from Earth to supply the demand for these thousands of different kinds of devices. And the devices we are making are so effective that some Earth people are wondering if they can get or make them, too. This latter deeply, deeply frightens many people and politicians on Earth. "What can these Martians be thinking! Has the radiation addled their brains?" is a common refrain in Earth media reports, and it isn't the comedy reports, either. The groundwork is being laid for a backlash.

A second big scary surprise is happening about the same time that nuclear concern is growing, but it is totally different. The second surprise is that Mars businesses are taking off like gangbusters. They are getting so successful, in fact, that there starts to be a labor shortage. Well, actually the labor shortage is nothing new—everyone always stays busy on Mars. What is new is that Martian businesses are contracting to do projects that previously had been done on Earth. I, for instance, find that once I am established, I can get all sorts of design projects from Earth contractors—many more than I can handle. And it is because I can charge less. At first I hire some Chinese to help. The business keeps growing, so I call in a couple of Argentinean designers who have come over with that geologist. We add a Martian tango line. And that still isn't enough. We are so busy!

Mars is becoming a faster, cheaper, more flexible human labor source.

This has happened for two reasons. First, travel technology is improving steadily. It is getting faster, cheaper, and easier to travel between Earth and Mars. Second, it is because, compared to everywhere on Earth, we are light on work regulations—if someone wants to take the work... why not? And once that is recognized, some people start coming to Mars not as colonists, not as tourists, but as contract laborers. These new workers apply to come to Mars as tourists, but when they get here, instead of staying at the conventional tourist hotels and doing conventional tourist activities, they stay in newly constructed dormitories in the working areas of the settlements and work. (We start calling these new residences motels.) They come to me, and I hire one or two for some rush projects. Then I hire some more…

In fact, we have to change the infrastructure growth plans for Mars quite a bit to put in more motel areas for these transient workers. It is quite strange. Technically they are tourists, and they will leave after a few months just like real tourists do. But you only see them for a day or two at real tourist attractions, usually after their assignments are completed and they are winding down. The rest of the time, they are total nerds, hovering over their work areas when awake and flopped in beds when not.

This transient worker population gets pretty large. When it grows to twice the colonial population and five times the real tourist population, some union leaders on Earth take notice and start complaining.

The tourist areas change a lot, too. The first ones—the pre-colonial ones—are expensive and highbrow, like the Marriott, and remain so. But as the traffic picks up, and the colonials respond to market demands, a bunch of first medium, then low-cost tourist facilities are developed along with the motels, which I don't count as tourist facilities.

The result of this market expansion is that the new tourist areas on Mars are transforming into border towns—the Amsterdam de Wallens, the Tijuanas, the Las Vegas Strips of Mars. In fact, some of the developers even borrow those names for what they create. Sigh! Not my favorite parts of Mars. What happens in these areas isn't like what happens elsewhere on Mars, and they have become even more "anything goes" places as time goes on.

It is another surprise. From the Earth moralist point of view, Mars is developing a vice industry. From the Mars colonist point of view, it is simply another form of the live-and-let-live, Mars isn't Earth, attitude. We let people pick their own way to be entertained, just like we let them pick their own way to work. The rest of us are all too busy to worry much about the details of how other people want to work and play.… As long as they bring money and don't kill us. Horsing around that causes property damage or otherwise endangers community safety is a harsh no-no on Mars. Earth-style property sabotage to make high-profile statements for political causes is not tolerated. Occasionally, those types come to Mars ready to make a statement. As soon as we get wind of it, they are hustled back to Earth, pronto! Nobody, but nobody, tolerates that kind of happy horseshit on Mars!

Which brings us to the Mars Independence Day Event.

Mars Independence Day

Between the nuclear proliferation (as Earthlings called it) and the motel dwellers and the border town tourist areas, Mars is stepping on a lot of Earth toes. And Earth people care. Mars is suffering more and more from the Curse of Being Important as the population and the economy grow.

In many ways, the Mars colony is an unparalleled success. It *does* grow. Its commerce grows so much that the shuttle fleet grows from one to ten ships and the communication bandwidth with Earth grows ten thousand-fold. Mars is now routinely creating stuff that has never been created on Earth. It is an exciting place. If Mars had any mineable gold, the streets would have been paved with it by now, and the projections as to when Mars' human population will hit a million are down to next year or the year beyond.

But the uproar on Earth is growing, too. Growing strong. An unholy alliance of unionists, baby watchers, nukephobes, and "Stick it to the Man" nomads forms and calls for tighter restrictions on how things are done on Mars. They want Mars regulations to be made by an Earth committee.

I guess I should mention that we have accidents, too. Annette dies the third year when one of the apprentice kids puts plug A into socket Z instead of socket B... thirty people die in that mishap. It is sad, and changes are made, but the Zion Club doesn't change their ways, and that gets a lot of Earth people upset.

"People are dying! It's clearly not working!" those outraged Earth people argue.

"What?" say the Zion people back. "We had accidents on Earth, and we have them here. What's not working?"

What becomes a shadow government on Earth is originally set up by a bunch of malcontent bloggers. They go through the motions of electing a legislature, which elects a president and a cabinet, and they then proceed to remotely pseudomanage affairs on Mars—they read the news feeds from Mars and blog about what laws and regulatory commissions Mars needs to fix its "problems" as reported by the news feeds, and then they set those up among their people on Earth.

The Earth media eats this up with a spoon. They start adding shadow government sound bites to their Mars coverage.

It is spooky for us colonials to watch. It gets even spookier when a couple of Earth politicians announce at their press conferences that they are consulting with this shadow government before they decide their policies on Martian affairs.

Our government protests when word of this gets to Mars, but those Earth pols just snark back, "Earth isn't Mars."

It gets serious when the money flow is affected.

This shadow government sets up a customs house in the Earth-side transfer station where the Mars shuttles dock. It is originally financed by some whacked out son-of-a-bi…llionaire who buys into this shadow government pap hook, line, and sinker. Once it is set up, it starts levying tariffs on goods coming from and going to Mars—tariffs decided by the shadow government's Tariff Commission, and that shadow government gets the revenues! It is just insane!

The Space Agency is blindsided. When it handed over sovereignty to the Mars government, it was supposed to become just another bureau on Earth that has transformed from running something into coordinating between the old and new sovereign entities. As this crisis grows, the people running the Space Agency simply duck.

The media and people of Earth look upon this as just more social hijinks by some protest group. They laugh it off. The media features it! We on Mars don't see any humor in this at all. Our government is being dissed. If this had been the 1700s, we would have been bringing out the muskets and dumping tea. As the Martian hotheads blog, "It's time to show Earth our government has a pair."

I sympathize, but we have to come up with something 22nd century, and that takes putting on some thinking-caps.

Being polite hasn't worked. Cooperating with the powers-that-be on Earth who handle commerce hasn't protected us from this humiliation. So it is time for some fighting fire with fire.

Anton is still on Earth, the creations still want to see Mars be a big success, and we have other followers, well-wishers, and wannabes as well. The Mars government consults with Anton. He advises against cutting off our noses to spite our faces. In this case that means any kind of retaliation boycott.

"There are plenty of angry people on Earth already. You don't need to add to that list," he says. "What you need to do is convince the Earth governments that by supporting this disrespecting of you, they are supporting the disrespecting of themselves. That will cut this nonsense off in a big hurry.

"And this may be arrangeable..."

So other than being verbally outraged, we have patience. We do a bit of name-calling, but mostly we just let those shadow government people hang themselves.

It takes a couple of months, but they do. They aren't any kind of real government, so those that stay with it evolve into a group of competing comedians making fun of current politics. And while that is happening, Anton is encouraging other malcontented bloggers to set up shadow governments of various Earth institutions.

When shadow DMV's start to show up offering ten minute service, and a shadow IRS on the Lincoln Memorial, and a shadow Tax Commission on Tiananmen Square, the Earth governments get the hint, and the customs house business is declared a prank and shut down. Likewise, many of the politicians now realize the fire they are playing with and move back to more conventional ways of making their talking points. The shadow government is a fad that fades.

And after the shadow government crisis, the Martians become pretty well respected for being Martians. We are different, and we are independent. We are also just the first. Earth-Mars commerce is now big enough to support many ships making profitable journeys. What comes next is more ships that go farther afield. Mars is just the first, and we Child Champs are real proud to have done our part to make it a hugely successful first.

We are now truly making babies—and humanity—in the 22nd century way.

THE
END